USTEN

BOY TROUBLE

SHERYL BERK
& CARRIE BERK

This is a work of fiction. Any references to historical events, real people, or real places are used fictitiously. Other names, characters, places, and events are products of the author's imagination, and any resemblance to actual events or places or persons, living or dead, is entirely coincidental.

251 Park Avenue South, New York, NY 10010

Manufactured in the United States of America MAP 1019
First Edition

1 3 5 7 9 10 8 6 4 2

Library of Congress Cataloging-in-Publication Data
is available upon request.
ISBN 978-1-4998-0649-6
yellowjacketreads.com

To Jordana, Kelly, Sierra, and the entire gang at Brandsway Creative. Love you all! Thank you for always believing in me–Carrie

1

THE COLD SHOULDER

“Guys, you have to see this text!”

Emma Woods sprinted up the steps of Austen Middle School, where her two best friends, Isabelle Park and Harriet Horowitz, were seated at the top waiting for her. Emma noted that even from several feet away, Izzy always looked so put together—her lime-green headband perfectly matched her velour tracksuit. As for Harriet, her mousy-brown hair could be a bit unruly at times, but today she'd put it in braids. They looked cute against a sweater embroidered with cheerful cherries. Emma hadn't given much thought to her own school outfit today—she had more important things on her mind. The air had a chill in it, so an orange sweatshirt, jeans, and a messy bun seemed a fine choice. In the sunlight on the school steps, her hair glowed auburn, *strawberry blonde* her mom liked to call it. When she reached her BFFs, she breathed a sigh of relief. They had been inseparable since kindergarten, even though they were all so different. It's what kept them excited to be friends. They never got bored together.

When Emma reached the top of the stairs, she waved her phone in the air. Izzy and Harriet instantly flew into protective mode. "It's not someone writing mean comments on your blog again, is it?" Izzy asked, delicately. When Emma had started her *Ask Emma* advice blog at Austen, some of her classmates had resented her butting into their lives. But fixing problems and giving advice was Emma's specialty—

it made her feel happy and whole and she was good at it. After a few months, she had not only won her peers over but she also developed quite a following. Her inbox was constantly flooded with kids asking her to help sort out their issues—everything from school problems and relationships to parents and poor self-esteem. Although this morning, *she* was the one who needed advice. It was always easy for her to see the perfect solution for someone else, but when it came to her own life, her vision could get fuzzy.

"If you're being bullied, you have to tell Principal Bates," Harriet told her. "Is someone picking on you again?"

"No, no, no," Emma assured them and took a seat. "I'm not being bullied. This text is supergood . . . I think. I don't know. Just read it!"

Emma held out her phone and the two of them huddled around her. Harriet read out loud:

"Meet for math homework tomorrow at Freddy's? I owe you money for lunch on the train home from DC, so I'll pay. See you soon."

The text was from Jackson Knight, a fellow seventh grader she had a major crush on. Emma couldn't believe he invited her to Freddy's Deep Freeze Ice Cream Shoppe, which indisputably made the best sundaes in all of New Hope, Pennsylvania. But she wasn't quite sure if this counted as their "first date." After all, they'd only admitted to liking each other a week ago after teaming up at the National Student Congress in Washington, DC. They'd spent so much time preparing their arguments and working together, dating just seemed like the logical next step. And this would be her very first boyfriend! But Jax definitely had a knack for keeping her guessing. Maybe it was what drew her to him in the first place—he was the new boy at Austen Middle and his air of mystery was exciting. That and his wavy black hair and sparkling blue eyes . . .

"So is he asking me out?" Emma looked at her friends. "Like, is it official?"

"Hmm," Harriet replied, trying not to burst Emma's bubble. "Well, it's polite of him to pay you back."

"It sounds like he needs help with pre-algebra," Izzy said. She always called it like she saw it. "I wouldn't read too much into it, Em."

But that was the point! Emma wanted to read more into it! She wanted to believe that the moment Jax asked her to dance at the Congress after-party and professed that he liked her wasn't all a fleeting dream.

"So it's not a date," Emma said, disappointed. "Why do you think he changed his mind so quickly? Is he having second thoughts? Cold feet?"

Harriet spied Jax climbing off the school bus dressed in a puffer jacket, ski hat, and scarf. "He looks pretty warm to me," she said.

Before Emma could think of a good comeback, Jax was climbing the stairs toward them.

"Hey," he said simply, stopping at the step beneath Emma.

She looked down and their eyes met. "Hey," she replied. Ugh! Why did her cheeks flush whenever she spoke to him?

"Freddy's after school, right?" he asked.

Emma stared at him, dreamily. Izzy had to elbow her in the ribs to answer. "Um, yeah. Sounds good."

"Great. See ya later!"

He raced past them into school just in time for the first bell to sound.

"He seemed enthusiastic," Harriet assured Emma as they scrambled to their feet. "Like he's really looking forward to it."

"Who wouldn't be looking forward to a Freddy's hot fudge sundae?" Izzy commented. Harriet shot her a look, and she added, "I mean, who wouldn't be looking forward to a sundae with his *girlfriend*?"

Girlfriend? Two seconds ago she was convinced he just needed help with a worksheet, but one smile and all of a sudden she was thinking about what their names would be if they got married. Would they hyphenate? Would she be Mrs. Emma Knight? What if he wanted her last name? Mr. Jax Woods. Dad would like that! She was laughing to herself, thinking about how confused her grandma would be, when she practically collided with Principal Bates in the school atrium.

"Oops! Sorry!" she said, stepping on Ms. Bates's toes.

"It's okay," the principal replied. "I have five more toes on the other foot. I hope you were distracted thinking about your next blog. I do look forward to *Ask Emma*'s posts."

"Um, yeah." Emma was relieved Ms. Bates had given her a good excuse for acting so spacey. "I got a really tricky question. I was just thinking of how I should respond."

"What's the question?" Ms. Bates asked her.

"Question?"

"The one that has you stumped?"

"Oh, *that* question!" Emma panicked. She didn't have a student question to answer, but she didn't want to talk to Ms. Bates about Jax. How embarrassing! She had to improvise.

"It's about a boy. And a girl. A girl who likes a boy."

"Uh-huh," Ms. Bates replied. "And does the boy like her back?"

"I think so. That's the question. It's not one hundred percent crystal clear."

"So what advice are you giving this girl?" Ms. Bates continued.

"I guess I'm telling her to give it time, wait and see how things go, take it slow. Just be yourself and be patient because relationships are complicated and they take time to grow. And don't act all weird and pushy—otherwise, I'll scare him off."

Ms. Bates raised an eyebrow. "*You'll* scare him off?"

"I mean *she'll* scare him off. That's what I mean."

Ms. Bates nodded. "Sounds like very good advice to me."

Now all Emma had to do was follow it!

"Well, I hope *she* gets what she wants. She sounds like a smart girl."

Ms. Bates winked and walked off leaving Emma standing in the atrium, stunned. Did she know about her and Jax? Did everyone at Austen Middle assume they were going to be a couple? And if they did, could someone *please* fill Jax in?

#

The day seemed to drag on forever—especially last period. Emma watched the clock on the classroom wall slowly tick until it reached 3 p.m.

"Gotta run!" she called to Harriet, who was still packing up her English notebook.

"Good luck!" Harriet shouted after her. "Text me later with all the details!"

When Emma arrived at her locker, Jax was leaning on it, waiting for her.

She smiled. "I'm all ready to walk to Freddy's!"

"Freddy's? I love Freddy's!" a voice suddenly interrupted. Elton appeared out of nowhere and elbowed right in between them. Emma was positive he didn't do it to be mean—they'd been friends since kindergarten. He was just kind of clueless when it came to couples. Actually, when it came to most things, besides sports and science and video games.

"The Super Quadruple Scooper Sundae is the best," Elton continued, ignoring her pleading look.

Jax nodded. "I know, right? With hot fudge?" They high-fived each other as Emma stood there impatiently tapping her foot. Then the conversation turned to the soccer match next Friday . . . and last night's episode of *American Ninja Warrior* . . . and some new video game Elton got. Emma was being completely left out.

"Ready?" she asked Jax again. How long could the two of them stand there talking about nothing?

"Huh? Oh, yeah," Jax replied. She took him by the elbow and steered him away from his track and soccer teammate before Elton could invite himself along.

"So," she said as they began strolling the six blocks to the center of town. Emma tried to walk close to Jax, hoping they might brush shoulders or accidentally touch hands, anything to make their walk feel special.

"So," Jax replied. "I'm kind of lost on the properties of operations problems."

Really? Was he seriously going to make small talk about math? Maybe he didn't want to date her after all. She needed to know for sure.

"I had so much fun in DC, didn't you?" She tried to remind him of how he had said he liked her—without actually having to remind him. She replayed his words in her head: *I've been wanting to ask you forever: Would you maybe like to go out with me sometime?* That's what he had said, so why was he talking about math when they finally had the chance to be together?

"The Washington Monument was awesome," Jax recalled. "I never realized how tall it was till I saw it in person."

Emma tried again: "And the party after the championship. I don't think I'll ever forget it."

"Yeah, I mean, who gets to see a private concert by Maroon 5?" Jax added. "That was sick."

Actually, Emma was starting to feel a little sick. This conversation was not going in the right direction. Under the bright lights of the competition, they were on the same page, but now . . . were they even in the same book?

#

They arrived at Freddy's, and Jax made his way past the counter and several tables covered in red gingham tablecloths to finally select a booth in the back that was private and quiet. Maybe that was a good sign?

Freddy, a plump, older gentleman with a white beard and glasses, greeted them. When she was little, Emma remembered how much he reminded her of Santa Claus. Freddy had been in the ice cream business for more than fifty years, and behind the counter, he kept a display of old ice cream scoops, fluted glass bowls, and the original sign that hung in the window when they first opened their doors. It read, FREDDY'S DEEP FREEZE IS READY TO PLEASE!

"Well, Emma, nice to see you," Freddy said, wiping his hands on his apron.

"You know the famous Freddy?" Jax whispered.

Emma nodded. "My dad's been coming here since he was three."

"That's right," Freddy said, grinning. "I remember your grandpa used to sit him up right on the counter and order him a root beer fizz. Your dad could polish off two or three of them in one sitting."

"Still can," Emma giggled.

"Well," Freddy continued, "what can I get for the two of you today?"

He handed them each a menu. There were so many interesting treats to choose from—and the most tempting, out-of-the-ordinary flavors.

"What is Chip-Chip Hooray?" Emma asked.

"That's my brand-new flavor creation," Freddy replied proudly. "Coffee ice cream with white and dark chocolate chips mixed in. But, if you ask me, the best flavor is Nuttin' Honey—it's honey vanilla with a swirl of chunky peanut butter."

Emma wrinkled her nose. "I don't love peanut butter. But the Earthquake Milkshake sounds interesting."

Freddy nodded. "It's got six different ingredients all swirled into a towering shake: chocolate fudge, caramel, mini marshmallows, toffee chips, fudge ripple ice cream, and chocolate milk."

Emma vetoed yet again. "Sounds too sweet."

"Maybe you need some more time?" Freddy suggested.

"We'll have the Kitchen Sink Split," Jax hurried to order for them. "One scoop of cookies and cream, one scoop of rocky road, one scoop of pistachio—"

Emma held up her hand. "Um, no pistachio. I hate it."

"You hate it? How could you hate it? It's my favorite flavor!" Jax exclaimed.

"It's green. Alien green."

"So? It tastes amazing."

"It tastes nutty," Emma said, wrinkling her nose. "Let's get a scoop of strawberry-banana instead."

"Strawberry-banana?" Jax dropped his menu on the table. "Seriously? Gross! It can't even make up its mind what fruit it is! I'm guessing you don't like hot fudge, either?"

Emma shook her head. "Not really. I mean, ice cream is supposed to be cold. Why would you ruin it by pouring something hot on it?"

"Chocolate sprinkles?" Jax asked.

"Actually, I like rainbow ones."

Freddy chuckled. "I think I'll just come back and take your order when you two work out your differences."

"Differences?" Emma protested. "We don't have differences."

"Really? Coulda fooled me. But nothing one of Freddy's famous sundaes can't solve!" The old man went to pour them two glasses of water.

"Do we?" Emma asked Jax quietly.

"Do we what?"

"Have differences. Stuff that we can't agree on?"

Jax shrugged. "Well, yeah. I mean, I'm me and you're you, Emma. We're two different people."

"But, if we can't agree on ice cream flavors, how are we supposed to, you know—"

Jax interrupted her: "I guess we could just order our own sundaes."

"I wasn't talking about sundaes. I was talking about *us*."

Jax's cheeks flushed. "Oh, *us*."

She waited for him to say something else. Anything else. Finally, he broke the silence.

"Do you think Ms. Bennet is going to give us a surprise quiz in math tomorrow? She seemed like she was hinting at it."

Emma was about to explode. She didn't want to talk about math! She wanted to discuss their relationship and the fun moments they'd shared in DC. Why was he changing the subject? If he liked her, why was he talking about homework? If he didn't like her, why had he just tried to split a sundae together? What was going on?!

"I have no idea if we're going to have a surprise quiz, Jax," she said with a huff. "That's the point. It's a surprise."

"Oh. Um. Well, let's just get our ice cream and then we can go over the chapter. I'm really lost."

When Freddy returned with their water, Jax blurted out his order: "So I'll have two scoops of pistachio ice cream with hot fudge and chocolate sprinkles."

"Sounds good!" Freddy said, cheerfully. Then he turned to Emma. "And what do you want, Emma?"

Emma rolled her eyes at Jackson. What she really wanted to say was "I want a boyfriend who doesn't flip-flop on how he feels about me!" Instead, she simply replied, "One scoop of strawberry-banana with rainbow sprinkles, please," and opened her math book.

#

As promised, Emma texted Harriet and Izzy as soon as she got home with all the details of her "date" with Jax.

He only wanted to talk about math! she typed and added a screaming face emoji for punctuation.

Boys! Izzy typed back with a frowning emoji.

Ugh! Harriet added with a poop emoji.

While she appreciated her friends' sympathy (and Harriet's sense of humor), it didn't solve anything. She was still left with the same perplexing problem: Why was Jax acting as if nothing had happened between them? Why was he treating her like a friend instead of a girlfriend? To distract herself, she decided to sign on to her advice blog and see if someone had a problem she *could* fix.

Dear Emma,

I like this boy and I've been thinking of telling him, but we are total opposites. He's all about skateboarding and horror movies and his pet iguana, and I like ballet and reading and photos of kittens. What if we have nothing in common? Can it ever work?

Sincerely,

Not His Type

Emma allowed her hands to hover over her laptop keyboard as she searched for just the right words to reply. She thought about her afternoon with Jax—then she took a deep breath and let her fingers fly:

Dear Not,

Have you ever heard the expression "opposites attract"? Don't let your hobbies hold you back from giving this relationship a try. I mean, maybe you won't always see eye to eye on stuff, and that's okay. You can complement each other—like peanut butter and jelly. Those two foods couldn't be more different (except for the sticky part), but most people (my brother in particular) would tell you they make a seriously perfect sandwich when you put them together. Or think of a magnet: Opposite charges always come together and like charges repel—if there's one thing I learned in sixth grade science, it's that. Stop worrying if you have nothing in common. Focus instead on what you like about him (and hopefully what he likes about you) and what it is that makes you smile whenever you think of him. The fact that you don't share a lot of interests could be a plus, and trying new things can be exciting and adventurous! If I were you, I would rather be in a relationship that challenges me and makes me think and push myself rather than one that's boring and same ol', same ol'. But hey, that's me. You have to make your own decisions. Just don't let doubts stand in the way of something potentially awesome.

XO,

Emma

She reread her response and hit the Send button so her advisor and computer teacher, Mr. Goddard, could approve and post it on the Austen seventh grade web page. Giving advice always made her feel better, and in this case, it made perfect sense for what had happened at Freddy's today as well. Maybe Jax was just as worried and freaked out as the girl who had written her this letter. Now that they were back in school with no more Student Congress prep, no more endless hours spent together preparing their debate arguments, he was probably terrified they would have nothing to say to each other. It was understandable, but then again, he should know her better by now.

She *always* had something to say.

2
INSTANT REPLAY

Friday was family movie night in the Woods household, and this time it was Emma's brother's chance to choose the film they all watched.

"Really? *Return of the Jedi*? Again?" their father complained as he plopped down on the couch with a bowl of popcorn. "Luc, could we please watch something different for a change?"

Luc shook his head. "You picked *Gandhi* last week

and Mom wanted *Gone with the Wind* the week before. And Emma always picks some sappy love story. It's my turn."

Emma groaned as the credits rolled across the screen: *A long time ago in a galaxy far, far away. . . .* Her big brother was so predictable. "You pick a *Star Wars* movie every single time it's your turn! I can recite this one by heart."

As the movie played for over an hour, Luc acted out each scene. He even picked up a pretzel stick and waved it in her face like a light saber. "I'll never turn to the dark side! Never!"

Mr. Woods chuckled. "You had to name him after Luke Skywalker," he said, teasing his wife.

"He's named after my great-uncle Lucian, remember?" Mrs. Woods replied.

Emma watched as Luc hit the rewind button on the TV remote control three times in a row.

"What are you doing?" she said, trying to wrestle it out of his hand. "Gimme that!"

"Nuh-uh," Luc insisted. "Skywalker is telling Emperor Palpatine he's failed in his quest to turn him to the forces of evil. Everyone be quiet!"

He played the line yet another time and recited along: "I'm a Jedi, like my father before me!"

"I thought I was a cardiologist, not a Jedi," Mr. Woods joked.

But Emma was losing her patience. "Seriously, Luc? This is ridiculous! Why do you have to play it over and over again?" She covered her head with a couch pillow to drown out the noise.

"Because it's *so good*," her brother insisted. "I want to hear every word."

While she was hiding her eyes, Emma actually had an idea. What if she could rewind what had happened between her and Jax in DC and play it back for him to jog his memory? There was no DVD of *Emma and Jax's Great Adventure*, but maybe there was another way. . . .

"I'm outta here," she said, tossing the pillow at Luc.

"Hey! No bailing on Family Movie Night," he reminded her. "I didn't walk out when you made us watch *To All the Boys I've Loved Before*—and it was putting me to sleep."

"First of all, I know you loved that movie. You can't fool me. Secondly, I'm not bailing, I'm just . . . taking a break. Mom, Dad . . . please can I go do something else?" Emma pleaded. "I know how this movie ends. I've seen it a gazillion times."

"Fine," Mr. Woods relented. "Only because we've *all* seen it a gazillion times."

"'So be it, Jedi,'" Luc said, quoting the film. "I will not fight you."

Emma raced upstairs to her room and took out her phone. She'd snapped tons of photos on their DC trip—why hadn't she thought of this before? She opened her computer and began uploading the images. There was the lobby of the hotel they had stayed in with all the other students. The photo showed Jax waving to her from a big red couch. Then there was a pic of the Lincoln Memorial—Jax had remarked that Lincoln had bigger feet than his! And finally, the skyscraping Washington Memorial, where they'd gazed up at the stars. It was a definite "moment" for her movie.

The video was coming together—she just needed

to add a soundtrack. She remembered how she and Jax had decided they would be an unstoppable team, and to calm his nerves, she told him to sing "We Go Together," from *Grease*. Well, that seemed like a perfect tune to play.

Luc knocked on her door, just as she was in the middle of editing. "I just wanted you to know you're missing the best scene in the entire movie," he told her.

Emma looked up. "Really? Which is one is that? The one where the green little muppet croaks?"

Luc scowled. "Do not make fun of Yoda. He's a very cool, very old dude." Then he squinted his eyes, hunched over and did his best Yoda impersonation. "'When nine hundred years old you reach, look as good, you will not.'"

"I definitely see the resemblance between you and Yoda," Emma teased. "The green pointy ears, the wrinkles . . ."

"What was so important that you had to skip out on *Return of the Jedi*?" Luc asked, curious to see what she was doing on her computer screen.

Emma slammed her laptop closed. "It's none of your beeswax."

"Oh. So this is about your major crush on Jackson Knight." He grinned and waited for Emma to react. Luc had a knack for knowing exactly what buttons to push—but she wasn't about to give him the satisfaction.

"Why are you such a know-it-all?"

"Why are you such a girl?" Luc shot back.

"Is that supposed to be an insult, Luc? If it is, you better be real careful with what you say next. Because I *am* a girl and I'm proud of it," Emma said.

"That's not what I meant," Luc said. "But let me give you a little piece of advice, not as your brother, but as a guy . . . and a Jedi."

Emma groaned. "Ugh, fine."

"You need to ease up. The more you push, the more you're gonna push this dude away."

"I'm not pushing," Emma insisted. "I'm just *reminding*. You actually gave me the idea hitting the Rewind button on the remote over and over again."

"Don't try and pin this on me! If your plan doesn't work, it's not my fault."

Emma knew that was true. She also knew she wasn't to blame. If Jax didn't want to go out with her, it was his choice and his loss. Besides, she wasn't the one who asked him to Freddy's; he had made the first move. Emma was just trying to make her feelings clear.

"Earth to Emma, come in, Emma?" Luc said, waving his hand in her face. "So are you coming downstairs to watch Yoda fade away? Mom just put brownies in the oven. The one with the M&M's in them. I know you love those."

"Okay, okay," she said, tossing aside her laptop. "I guess I'm pretty much done, anyway."

"Wise you are," Luc put on his Yoda voice again. "And wise it is to let the boy be."

Emma wasn't about to let Luc in on her plan, or on her little secret: She actually *loved* Yoda. After all, he was just like her—a little person who loved to give advice.

#

On Monday morning, Emma filled Izzy and Harriet in on her plan to get Jax over to her house for a trip down memory lane. She showed them a sneak peek of her movie on her phone.

"Aw," Harriet gushed. "I love the selfies! And that pic of you guys dancing in the ballroom—I took that when we were hiding behind the chocolate fountain watching you! Well, I was watching. Izzy was more focused on filling a water pitcher with chocolate to take back to the room."

Izzy shrugged. "What can I say? I know how to party."

Emma smiled. "Everything that night was so perfect."

"Except for the fact that you guys came in second," Izzy reminded her. "You were robbed."

"But we came in second *together,*" Emma replied, dreamily.

Harriet took off her glasses and wiped them on

the corner of her sweater. "Do you really think Jax is confusing you on purpose? I mean, maybe he just has a really bad memory and forgot everything that happened in DC. Don't you remember that one time in second grade when Izzy fell off the monkey bars and bumped her head and thought you were me and I was you?"

Izzy laughed out loud. "Harriet, I was kidding. It was a joke. You actually believed I forgot your name?"

Harriet looked shocked. "Are you kidding me? I totally believed you! I wore a name tag to school for a week!"

Emma knew that being forgetful wasn't Jax's problem. He could memorize a gazillion historical facts and never forget a single one. He actually quoted her Lincoln's Gettysburg Address when they visited the president's monument: "Fourscore and seven years ago our fathers brought forth, on this continent, a new nation . . ." He sounded so confident reciting the speech on the steps overlooking the Mall. It was a moment she had etched in her memory forever.

"Nope, no way. I don't believe he has amnesia. He knows what he said to me in DC. He's just blocking it out for some reason. Like when Luc says he 'forgot' to pick up his smelly socks and sweats off the bathroom floor. My mom calls it 'selective amnesia.'"

"So you think your video will snap him out of it?" Izzy asked.

"I hope so," Emma said. "I hope he likes it." She also hoped she could get him to agree to come over to her house to watch it! "I need a reason for him to stop by today after school—a good one."

"Your mom's oatmeal raisin cookies?" Harriet suggested. "That would get me to come over."

Emma shook her head. "No, I'll think of a really great reason, one that he wouldn't suspect."

The solution presented itself during first-period math class. Ms. Bennet announced they would be having a unit test at the end of the week. Jax had math later in the day, and he was sure to freak out. It was just the drama Emma needed to set her plan in motion.

She found Jax at the water fountain with Elton, talking about a YouTube video of a kid with toilet paper stuck to his shoe that had gone viral.

"Oh, man, it cracks me up," Elton said. "How did he not notice? It was like a mile long!"

Jax laughed. "He dragged it all the way down the stairs—and across the street!"

"Ahem." Emma cleared her throat. "Big math test Thursday," she told Jax, cheerfully. "Huge. Entire unit. All those properties of operations questions you hate."

Jax's mouth fell open. "What? How do you know?"

"Ms. Bennet told us first period."

Elton shrugged. "So that's why she canceled the pop quiz. She was gonna hit us with a unit test instead."

Emma nodded. "Sneaky. Very sneaky. I guess I'll be studying after school so I make sure to maintain my A average in math class . . ." She looked at Jax; he was staring into space, utterly blindsided by the news. She knew he was barely getting a B.

"Um, maybe we could study together, Emma?" he asked her.

"You think that would be a good idea?" she said, batting her eyelashes. "I don't know. I kind of study better on my own."

"No! I mean, we were a great team in DC, right?" Jax reminded her.

She practically had to cover her mouth to stifle a laugh—*now* he remembered!

"I guess," she said, coyly. "If you really want to work together."

"I do!" Jax insisted. "I think we should start right away. Today."

Emma tapped a finger to her chin. "Let me see, what do I have going on after school today?" Jax was hanging on her every word. "Well, I told my mom I would take our dog, Jagger, out for a long walk. He really needs the exercise."

"Can't Jagger wait till after the unit test is over?" Jax pleaded.

"I suppose Luc could walk him," Emma replied. "If it's really that important to you."

"Dude, you could always come to my house after school and study," Elton suddenly offered. "I'm pretty good in math."

Emma wished she had some toilet paper from that YouTube video to stick in Elton's mouth! "No! Your house has way too many distractions!" she insisted. "Jax wants to study, not play video games."

Before Elton could say another word, Emma sealed the deal: "I'll meet you at our lockers at three ten sharp," she told Jax. "Operation Ace the Math Test commencing."

#

Walking home from school that day with Emma, Jax did a very good job of staring at his sneakers and not saying much—except for a quick weather report.

"Did the meteorologist say it was going to rain?" The wind whipped his hair in his eyes and the sky looked an ominous shade of dark gray. "I hope track practice isn't rained out tomorrow morning."

Emma stopped walking and waited for Jax to realize she was standing still, arms crossed, several feet behind him.

"Huh? Where'd you go?" Jax replied, puzzled. He walked back to stand next to her.

"Oh, you noticed?" Emma huffed. "I didn't think you had anything much to say to me."

"Emma, you're imagining things," Jax insisted. "I have plenty to say to you."

"Like what?" Emma pressed.

"Like, if we study all afternoon for the math test I know we'll both get an A."

Emma scowled. "There you go again! The most you have to say to me is about the weather or math. What happened to all of those deep conversations we had, about our hopes and dreams and the stuff that we had in common?"

Jax raised an eyebrow. "Is that what's bugging you? That I haven't told you about my dreams lately?"

His tone sounded sarcastic. Why didn't this matter to him? Emma fumed. "What's bothering me is that you're not interested in being my friend—which clearly you were in Washington, DC. Ever since we got back, you've acted like a different person."

"I'm sorry, but I just need to be really careful about managing my time." Jax tried to defend himself. "I literally just moved here. I'm on the soccer and track teams, and that's a lot of pressure on top of all my tests and homework."

"And I wouldn't understand because I don't have anything going on?" Emma tossed back.

"That's not what I mean! But sometimes you're just . . . never mind."

Emma took a deep breath. "Just what, Jackson?"

"I don't know. Sometimes, it feels like you just have to have everything *exactly* your way."

Emma was shocked. First, her brother accused her of being controlling, now Jackson. Tears started welling up in her eyes. She never thought Jackson would make her feel this way. "I think we should cancel today's study session," she finally said. "I want to be alone."

"Come on, Emma," Jax said, hiking his backpack up on his shoulders. "I didn't mean it like that."

But Emma couldn't even respond. For days she had been trying so hard to give Jackson her time and attention. But no matter what she did, it was wrong. The frustration built up inside of her chest and she didn't know whether she wanted to scream or cry. She hurried down the street leaving him standing by himself. Emma knew one thing: She didn't want to be around Jax right now. And that feeling was a first. In a matter of minutes, their entire relationship—and her great plan—had just imploded.

3
LADIES FIRST

"Nuh-uh. You just left?!" Harriet gasped as Emma recounted over an emergency call what had gone down between her and Jax on the walk home.

"I did," Emma admitted. "It was awful. I was just so mad at him."

"I can't believe it," Izzy weighed in. "He insulted you!"

"Who does he think he is?" Harriet said, outraged.

"But he was different in DC," Emma recalled. "He was so sweet and supportive. But now, even when it's just the two of us, I don't feel important to him."

"Em, you've got to accept reality," Izzy insisted. "Maybe Jackson is just fickle. He's changing his mind like Harriet changes her cat Romeo's kitty litter."

"Oh, and that's every day, sometimes even twice a day," Harriet chimed in. "Romeo likes a tidy litter box."

"So, that's it?" Emma tried to process what they were saying. "Our relationship ends before it even begins? Am I'm supposed to forget everything we said to each other? Everything we meant to each other at the Student Congress?"

Izzy considered. "Maybe. At least for now. You just focus on you and let him go off and do his thing."

Emma mulled over her friends' advice. She knew it was probably the smartest, sanest decision she could make about her relationship with Jax. But that didn't mean it didn't hurt . . . a lot.

"I just miss *us,*" she said quietly.

"Maybe this isn't forever," Harriet said, trying to

cheer her up. "Maybe it's just a temporary hiatus. Like how my fave TV show *The Zombie Chronicles* takes a little break over the summer and comes back in the fall with new episodes?"

Emma felt like crying. "We're not zombies. And I don't know what I would do if Jax didn't talk to me until next fall."

"Maybe he just needs to miss you like you miss him," Izzy said, thoughtfully. "How does that saying go, 'Absence makes the heart grow bigger'?"

"Fonder," Emma corrected her. "It's supposed to make the heart grow fonder."

"So wave your hands in the air like you just don't care," Izzy advised. "Buh-bye, Jax. I bet he'll come running back to you."

Emma thought for a moment: "You really think he'll come back?"

"He'd be crazy not to," Harriet agreed. "You're a really great person who cares about everyone and always tries to be kind. He just doesn't realize how amazing you are. It's like the time my kitty, Romeo, ran away from home. I was worried sick! But, the next day, he realized he missed me scratching him behind his ears and feeding him his cans of tuna. He came home and never left again."

"So, the moral of this story is to make sure you stock up on tuna," Izzy teased, trying to make her BFF chuckle. "Though I'm not sure how much Jax would like being scratched behind the ears."

"I'm not sure what he likes these days," Emma said, ignoring the joke. "But it sure seems like he doesn't like me."

Emma had a hard time that night focusing on her homework or even any of the questions waiting for her in her inbox. But, as bad as she felt, she knew someone in her grade was also troubled and needed her advice. She opened an email and began to read it:

> Dear Emma,
> This girl I really like has a birthday coming up, and I want to get her a present that will really wow her so she'll like me back. But here's the problem: I'm totally broke. When

I last checked, I had only thirty-three cents in my backpack. I need to earn some money, but what can a kid who's only thirteen do?

Signed,

Down on Dollars

Emma's dog, Jagger, came into her room carrying a tennis ball in his mouth and climbed up on her bed. "No drooling on my laptop," she warned him. But it also gave her an idea of what to write:

Dear Down,

I don't have to remind you that when it comes to gift giving, it's the thought that counts, right? Why are you determined to buy her some crazy expensive present? She should like you for being you—not because you handed her a little blue box from Tiffany's. That said, I'm all for being an entrepreneur and earning money—and I have a few suggestions. Why not start a dog-walking biz on your block? Personally, my dog wants to go out all the time, and I bet he's not alone. Ask some neighbors if you can take their pooches out for exercise and in turn, they will pay you (and not in doggie treats). Or you could pick up a paper delivery route like my brother, Luc, did when he was younger. Fair warning, though: he had to get up at 6 a.m. six days a week. Because he's now a teenager and needs his beauty sleep, he got a new job at Partytopia after school. I'm sure that will come in handy for my dad's upcoming 40th birthday—they sell party hats, balloons, and candles shaped like golf tees! If party supplies aren't your thing, you could always do what I do—babysit! Just make sure you're cool with changing diapers and watching *Sesame Street*. If you're good in a subject, you could tutor, and if you've got a green thumb, you could help garden or mow people's lawns. I hope that gives you some ideas on how to score more cash. Good luck!

XO,

Emma

#

Principal Bates rarely called a seventh-grade assembly that wasn't scheduled—unless she had some big news she needed to convey. When the announcement came over the loudspeaker the next afternoon summoning all students to a last period meeting in the auditorium, Emma couldn't imagine what could be so urgent. Did someone doodle all over the girls' bathroom wall again? Were all the dodge balls in the gym deflated? Had the Animal Rights Club set the frogs free in the science lab?

Elton caught up to her outside the auditorium doors. "The rumor is there's a tater tot shortage," he informed Emma. "They ran out of them at second-period lunch and everyone was freaking out."

"I doubt that would make Ms. Bates hold a grade-wide assembly," Emma said. Then again, you never could tell with their principal—sometimes she just got a bee in her bonnet. "Was she really mad about it?" she inquired.

Elton nodded. "Oh, yeah. She had to step between

two sixth graders who were trying to wrestle the last one out of each other's hand. It got ugly."

Well, Emma reasoned, maybe this *was* about a war over tater tots. That was certainly fixable: just buy more! Then she saw Ms. Bates stroll by and march into the auditorium with a huge smile on her face. This was not the look of a principal with a potato problem.

"Okay, maybe I'm wrong," Elton reconsidered. "She looks pretty happy. Which means we're in for it. Big-time."

As the students filed in, Emma found a seat in the back with Izzy and Harriet. She saw Elton sit down a few rows in front of her, right next to Jax and their soccer teammates.

"Still hasn't apologized to you, huh?" Izzy whispered.

"He hasn't even *looked* at me," Emma replied. "It's like I'm invisible."

Ms. Bates tapped on the microphone and called for everyone's attention. "Ladies and gentlemen, please settle down." She motioned to Mr. Goddard, who hit a button on his laptop. An image of a comic-book character popped up on the screen behind her.

"May I introduce Sadie Hawkins," Principal Bates said, pointing to a cartoon of a barefoot girl wearing denim shorts. "She's a character in the Li'l Abner comic strip of the 1930s. She's quite famous for getting her man—and she's the namesake of Austen Middle School's first ever Sadie Hawkins Dance."

Elton's hand shot up. "Does that mean that we all get to dress up as our favorite comic-book characters? I call dibs on the Green Lantern."

Ms. Bates sighed. "No, not exactly. A Sadie Hawkins Dance is traditionally a social gathering where girls ask boys to go with them."

Harriet gulped and grabbed Emma's arm. "*Girls* ask boys? So I have to ask Marty?" It was a given that Harriet would invite the boy she was crushing on in science class—but she didn't have the slightest idea how to go about it. "Do I call him? Ask him in person? Send him a text? An email? A postcard?"

The auditorium began to buzz nervously.

All around her, Emma could hear her classmates panicking and posing endless questions: "What if a girl asks me and I don't wanna go—I hate dancing!" "Wait! What if more than one girl asks me?" "I have to ask a boy out? I've never even been on a date!" "If I take a boy to the dance, does that mean I have to buy him a corsage?"

Principal Bates clapped her hands together. "Quiet! Quiet! I know you all have lots of questions, which is why I called this assembly. While it might be fun for the girls to do the asking, it's also perfectly fine for anyone to attend alone or with a group of friends. We want everyone to participate. The event will be held in three weeks in the school gymnasium—"

"Ooh! Ooh!" Jordana Fairfax practically leapt out of her front-row seat. "The Austen cheerleading squad volunteers will be in charge of decorating!"

Ms. Bates forced a smile. "Lovely. Thank you, Jordana, for interrupting me with that generous offer."

"I'm thinking pink streamers, pink balloons, pink

tablecloths," Jordie continued. Her minions Lyla and Saige nodded their heads enthusiastically. "Pink for girl power!"

Izzy elbowed Emma. "So, if girls do the asking, maybe you should ask Jax?"

Emma's eyes grew wide. Ask him? Now? After his whole cold-shoulder act? "I can't," she said simply.

"Can't?" Izzy pressed. "Or won't? Emma, it's the perfect opportunity to see once and for all how he feels about you. You take the reins—like Sadie Hawkins."

"Who are you asking, Iz?" Harriet interrupted her.

"Yeah, Iz." Emma was relieved to change the subject. "Who are you inviting to the Sadie Hawkins Dance?"

Izzy smiled. "Well, isn't that obvious? I'm captain of the girls' gymnastics team. Elton is captain of the boys' soccer team. It's kind of a given that we go together."

Emma's jaw dropped. "Elton? I had no idea you liked Elton!"

Izzy shrugged. "I'm not exactly sure I *like* him, but

he's really athletic and a great team player just like me. Besides, it's no biggie—we've been friends since kindergarten."

So both her BFFs had a plan for the Sadie Hawkins Dance—which left Emma feeling even worse about the Jax situation than she did before. As the assembly ended, she watched the cheerleaders huddle around Jordie, who was no doubt doling out orders. But then Elton and Jax joined their group.

"Ugh! What is she doing talking to them?" Izzy said, noticing. "Elton's *my* date."

"Technically, he's not," Harriet pointed out. "You haven't asked him yet."

Emma watched as Jordie giggled and rested her hand on Jax's shoulder. Double ugh.

"Okay, you need to go do something about this," Izzy said, giving Emma a shove in Jordie's direction.

"Me? Why should I do it?"

Izzy placed her hands on her hips. "Why? Because you're Miss Fixer-Upper Ask Emma, that's why!"

Well, if she put it that way . . .

"Jordie!" Emma called. She approached the front of the auditorium where the queen bee was holding court.

The smile faded from Jordie's face. "What do you want, Emma?"

"To help you—with whatever you need for the decorating committee."

"That's so funny," Elton said. "Jordie was just asking if she could come over to my dad's hardware store this afternoon and pick up a few things."

So she *was* trying to rope Elton into helping her—Izzy was right! Jax was pretending to be disinterested in the conversation but suddenly spoke up. "That works for me, Jordie. I can be there and help you carry stuff home."

So now she had sucked Jax in, too? Emma had to think fast.

"Did I mention that my brother works after school at Partytopia?" Of course! Why hadn't she thought of that sooner?! "I'm sure he can get you a discount on whatever you need for the dance: balloons, streamers, giant cardboard hearts. And they do free setup and even rent a confetti cannon."

Jordie's face lit up. "Really? That would be amazing! The more confetti the better." She turned to Elton. "Thanks, but I think we have it all under control. We won't be needing your help." She dismissed them with a wave of her hand.

Phew, Emma thought, that was a close one.

"Meet us there at four thirty," Jordie instructed her. "I'll have a long list of Sadie Hawkins must-haves."

Izzy was waiting outside the auditorium for her. "Thanks, Em," her friend said, gratefully. "Whatever you did, it worked. When Jordie left, she didn't seem to have any interest in Elton anymore."

Emma wasn't sure what she had promised Jordie—only that it would probably make Luc furious at her. She went straight to Partytopia after school so she could smooth things over with her brother before the demanding cheer squad arrived.

"Emma! I only started working here two weeks ago!" Luc said. He was standing behind the counter, dressed in a red shirt that read, THE FUN STARTS HERE!, and a polka-dot party hat. "You're gonna get me fired!"

"Don't be silly," Emma said—then realized that was impossible given what he was dressed in. "Jordie is going to buy a ton of stuff for the dance and make you look like an expert salesperson."

Luc considered. "How much is a ton?"

"Whatever she asks for, tell her she needs more, more, more," Emma advised him. "Jordie's motto in life is 'you can never have too much.'"

When the girls arrived, Jordie immediately sent them all scampering for shopping carts. "Where is your pink section?" she asked Luc with not so much as a "hello" or introduction. "I have a very specific décor design in mind." She handed him a sketch, all drawn in pink Magic Marker.

"Follow me," he said, guiding them to a long aisle filled with every pink paper good and party supply imaginable. On one shelf, there were pink plates, cups, napkins, tablecloths, streamers, centerpieces, balloons, and plastic utensils. On the other were pink hats, party horns, boas, and boxes of twinkly lights.

"We have seventy students in the grade," she said, checking her list.

"I think you'll want double that amount for everything," Luc corrected her. "Unless you want your guests to be underwhelmed."

Jordie pursed her lips. "I want them to think this is the biggest, best party Austen Middle School has ever thrown," she said. "Because I'm in charge of making it pretty and pink."

She pointed at Emma. "You said they have confetti cannons."

"We do!" Luc jumped in. "Do you want large, extra large, or jumbo parade size?"

"What do you think?" Jordie said. It was a rhetorical question. "I want a cloud of confetti. Actually, make that a tornado."

"One confetti twister coming up!" Luc said. His fingers could hardly keep up with tallying all the supplies Jordie needed. "Will that be all?"

"For now," Jordie said. "I'll give you my dad's

credit card. Make sure everything is delivered to Austen the day of the dance."

"Oh, Luc will deliver it personally and set it all up with his merry little Partytopia elves," Emma teased her brother. He actually didn't seem to care that she was making fun of him; he was too busy totaling Jordie's giant bill.

"I bet I'll get a bonus for this!" he whispered to Emma.

Jordie handed him the credit card and snapped her fingers for Lyla, Saige, and the rest of her squad to line up at the checkout. "Well, that was certainly exhausting!" she said. Emma noted that she hadn't pushed a cart or lifted a single item off a shelf.

"Good idea, Emma," Jordie said, patting her on the back.

Jordie and her crew were happy; Luc was over the moon. All in all, it had been a very successful day.

4

UP, UP, AND AWAY

Emma always checked her email at least twice a day to see if her peers had written to her with any perplexing problems—once before school, and once when she got home before she started her homework. She wanted to check more often, but her parents insisted if she got too "involved" with her blog and it interfered with her schoolwork, she'd have to give it up. So twice a day seemed a reasonable compromise—even if she did sneak a peek a few more times just in case. Most days there were a handful of questions—maybe three or four—that she would dutifully sift through and answer each Monday and Friday in her *Ask Emma* blog posts.

When she got home from Partytopia, she sat down on her bed and logged in to her Austen Middle School email account expecting one or two messages waiting for her since 8 a.m.—but this time the number next to her inbox read "29."

"Twenty-nine?" Emma gasped, paging down through them. "What is all of this?" She liked to feel needed, but this was a bit much! Each seemed to have a similar subject line: *Sadie Hawkins Dance HELP!; Sadie Hawkins SOS!; 911! Sadie Hawkins emergency!* She figured that a few girls would be stressing over which boys to ask, but she had no idea they would turn to her—or do it so quickly.

"Emma, I desperately need your advice!" read one message. *"I know who I want to ask to the dance, but I'm not sure how to go about it. I mean, are you supposed to give a boy flowers or chocolates and get down on one knee?*

Honestly, that's what I would like. . . ."

"If I ask him and he says no, does that mean I should ask someone else . . . or is that just not cool?" wrote another girl in her grade.

"What if I ask and he laughs in my face," wrote yet another. *"I'd be mortified!"*

Emma leaned back on her pillows and tried to concentrate. How could she possibly answer each and every one of these questions? She took a deep breath, let her fingers hover a few seconds over her laptop keyboard, and then began to type:

> Dear Seventh Grade Girls Stressing Out Over Sadie Hawkins,
>
> Judging from the truckload of questions I received today, you could use a little guidance on how to ask a guy to the upcoming dance. I'm not sure I'm an expert on the matter; I've never actually asked a boy out, so we're all in the same boat. That said, I do know how I would go about it.
>
> First off, I would think about how to make

it special and personal—not just "Hey, ya wanna go to the dance with me?" Have some fun with it and make it creative. For example, maybe he has a fave candy. You could make a card spelling out "I'm nuts about you!" in peanut M&M's and give it to him. Or maybe he's obsessed with sports. Scribble "Let's have a ball at the dance!" on a basketball in Sharpie and dribble it up to him.

Second, be sincere. Think about why this person is nice/smart/cool/great, etc. There has to be a reason you're choosing him over all the other boys in school, and I'm sure he'd like to hear it. (Who doesn't like a compliment?) Speak from your heart and be yourself. I always find I get my point across better if I brainstorm and jot down a few thoughts ahead of time—that way, my tongue doesn't get all tied up. I might even rehearse it with my two besties (who are really good at giving me feedback). I also highly recommend talking to some of his friends about your plan first. Go ahead and ask them: "Do you think he would be

into going with me? Does he already have a date lined up?" Better you know sooner rather than later, don't you think?

Lastly, I have one piece of advice for the boys (because I know you'll probably be writing me for advice next when the girls start asking!): Be kind. When girls put their hearts on the line, you shouldn't trample all over them. You should remember that we have feelings, and telling you how we feel about you can be really scary. You don't have to say yes when we ask you to the dance, but if it's a no, let us down easy. If a boy were going to reject me, I would hope he would do it politely and compassionately, not simply ice me out of his life with little or no explanation. I mean, who does that?

So there you have it. My two cents on Sadie Hawkins. Good luck, girls. I'm here if you need me.

XO,

Emma

As soon as she had finished typing up her post, her phone rang.

"Em, I need your help!" It was Harriet and she sounded very stressed out—even more than she had been at the afternoon's assembly.

"Oh, no, not you, too," Emma groaned.

"What do you mean? 'Not you, too'?"

"My email is overflowing with girls who need help with the Sadie Hawkins situation," Emma explained.

"Well, I'm your BFF. I should get a front-of-the line pass."

Emma chuckled. "Okay, you can skip to the front of the line. What's going on?"

"Like I told you in assembly, I'm not sure how to ask Marty, and I don't want to do it all wrong. I mean, should it be face-to-face? I might get all red, or break out in hives, or worse, faint from anxiety. Can't I just send him a text?"

"It definitely needs to be done in person," Emma advised. "And it has to be personal. What does Marty like?"

"Me, hopefully," Harriet replied.

"Besides you. What are his hobbies? His passions?"

"Well, we went to Comic Con together. He has this huge collection of comic books, hundreds of them—*Spider-Man, Batman, The Hulk, Captain America.* Oh, and he looked really cute in his Superman costume."

"Then that's it!" Emma exclaimed. "You need a superhero-worthy invite. Something that will really wow him. How would Supergirl do it?"

"She'd probably swoop down from the sky and hand him an invitation," Harriet considered. "Just one small problem: I don't fly."

"Yet," Emma said. An idea was starting to take shape—she could feel it. "You don't fly *yet*."

"Uh-oh. Whatever crazy scheme you're thinking of, if it involves my feet leaving the ground, it's a no. I don't like heights."

"Harriet, have I ever led you wrong?"

"I don't have to remind you of the Crisco catastrophe, do I?" Harriet said.

No, she didn't. Her parents had grounded her

for a week. "You said you wanted your scooter to go faster," Emma recalled. "How was I supposed to know the oil would make the wheels go so fast you'd fly off?"

"Three stitches in my head!" Harriet was still angry over the incident that happened five years ago. "I have a scar over my eyebrow, and that tree in my neighbor's yard always leans to one side from me hitting it."

"It was second grade," Emma assured her. "I promise not to use any cooking oil in my plan to help you get Marty. Unless the harness on the wire is a little squeaky . . . you don't want to get stuck up in the air."

"Harness? Wire? Up in the air?" Harriet's voice was now trembling. "Emma, what are you thinking?"

"You'll just have to wait and see," Emma said.

#

Emma knew that Harriet would be devastated if Marty turned her down, so she had to make her plan work. Being rejected was a horrible feeling—she knew this firsthand, and not just because of Jax. Her classmates had initially rejected her advice blog before they accepted her help. Ms. Bates had originally rejected her as a candidate for the National Student Congress before she agreed she would do a great job. Then there was the sixth-grade musical, the first time she had faced major rejection in her middle school career. As a soloist in the Austen Show Choir, Emma thought she was a shoe-in for the lead in *Peter Pan*—the audition had gone well and she'd belted out "I Won't Grow Up" with confidence and perfect pitch. Then Ms. Otto pulled her aside and explained her casting choice.

"We need someone who can handle doing somersaults in the air," the choir director explained. "Jordie does a lot of tumbling on the cheerleading squad—"

"But she only sings in the ensemble. I had solos in the fall and holiday showcases!" Emma insisted. "I sang the whole first verse of 'Scarborough Fair'!

Parsley, sage, rosemary, and thyme! That wasn't easy to memorize."

"You have a lovely voice, Emma," Ms. Otto told her. "And I'm not saying you don't deserve a large role in the show. I think you'd make a wonderful Wendy Darling."

Emma frowned. "The show is called *Peter Pan*. Not Wendy Darling." But she agreed to be a good sport and didn't complain when Jordie soared high over her head, crowing in the spotlight. Everyone loved Peter Pan; he was fun and fearless. Wendy just whined and scolded her brothers and the rest of the Lost Boys. And she wore a nightgown the entire show—also not a lot of fun. Peter wore tights and a feathered cap and carried around his shadow. It was so not fair.

She remembered the student who operated that spotlight and rigged the harness to safely support Jordie for three standing-room-only performances: Winston Bingley. Winston didn't say much; he mostly hung out backstage and made sure everything ran smoothly. But for what Emma was planning for Harriet, he would be the star of her scheme!

"Let me get this straight," Winston said after Emma had explained the whole situation. "You want me to hook Harriet up to a harness and fly her over the stage for what purpose?"

"So she can be Supergirl and ask Marty to go with her to the Sadie Hawkins Dance." Emma grinned; to her, the entire thing made perfect sense.

"And she couldn't just—oh, I don't know—email him?" Winston suggested.

"That's way too impersonal and incredibly unsuperheroey. I mean, how could Marty possibly say no when Harriet goes to all this trouble to invite him?"

Winston rubbed his temples. "And I suppose you have a Supergirl costume for her to wear? Costuming is an important part of every performance."

"Not yet. But I have Izzy on it," Emma replied. "All we need now is for you to say yes to helping Harriet take flight."

"And if I don't?" Winston asked. He pushed his glasses up on the bridge of his nose. "Will you keep bugging me until I do?"

"Yup, night and day," Emma promised. "So you might as well just give in now."

Winston sighed. "Fine. But let's keep this short and snappy. I don't want to get in trouble with Ms. Otto for hijacking her Peter Pan harness without permission."

"We will be in and out—faster than you can say Tinker Bell," Emma vowed. "We're thinking next Monday right after Marty's Lego Robotics Club meeting. I'll get him to come to the auditorium, you hit the stage lights, and then zoom Harriet right into his arms. Isn't it so romantic?"

Winston winced. "It sounds dangerous. I remember that Harriet wasn't exactly the most coordinated person in the show."

Okay, maybe she had tripped a couple of times onstage and knocked over Nana's doghouse. It could happen to anyone.

"So, whaddaya say, Winston?" Emma pushed.

"Are you willing to help Harriet wing it?"

"Fine," Winston said. "It's not like I have a choice, is it?"

"Nope!" Emma said, smiling. She left him moping in the Drama Club room and raced to find Harriet and Izzy who were waiting for her at her locker.

"We're a go," she told them both, excitedly. "Winston said yes."

"And I've got an old blue gymnastics leotard that will be perfect for your Supergirl costume," Izzy said. "I'll sew a red *S* on the front, and you can borrow my red miniskirt to go with it."

Emma and Harriet looked at each other—then at Izzy. "You sew?" they exclaimed in unison. To her friends, Izzy didn't seem at all the industrial arts type.

"If you must know, yes, I sew," Izzy admitted. "And I knit and crochet, too. Sometimes I'm sitting around for hours at a gymnastics meet waiting my turn. It's a great way to pass the time and calm my nerves."

"I make rainbow loom bracelets," Harriet

volunteered, not wanting to be upstaged.

"Guys, focus!" Emma snapped. "What about boots and a cape? Supergirl isn't Supergirl without her super accessories."

"It's all under control," Izzy assured her. "I'll dig through my little sister's dress-up trunk. I'm sure she's got a princess cape in there somewhere."

"And I have an old pair of red ladybug rain boots," Emma recalled. "That should work."

Harriet shrugged. She wasn't sure this was the best way to go about asking Marty to the dance, but Emma seemed positive that her plan was infallible.

"You get to the auditorium on Monday at three thirty and get in your costume and Winston will set you up on the harness. I'll get Marty in there at three forty-five sharp. What could go wrong?"

Izzy and Harriet looked at each other, then at Emma. "Do you want a list of things?" Izzy teased. "Marty could be early, Harriet could be late, the harness could snap—"

Emma put her hand over her friend's mouth. "We are going to think happy thoughts—just like Peter

Pan instructs the Darling children. That's all it takes."

"I played Nana the nursery dog," Harriet reminded her. "You're leaving out the part about needing pixie dust to get up, up, and away."

Izzy cracked up. "Great! So now we need to kidnap a fairy and have her work her magic on Harriet."

"Fairies aren't real, but love is," Emma said, placing an arm around Harriet. "I promise you Marty isn't going to know what hit him!"

5
IT'S A BIRD, IT'S A PLANE . . . IT'S HARRIET!

By Monday, Emma had rehearsed her plan several times with her BFFs and Winston. Harriet was slightly terrified every time her feet left the ground, but Winston convinced her it was all perfectly safe—and Izzy just told her to close her eyes and keep them shut. All that remained was to lure Marty into the auditorium without him suspecting anything.

Emma waited patiently for the Robotics Club to

wrap up their weekly meeting. Everyone came out of the room, except Marty. He was busy fidgeting with a pile of Legos and a small battery pack.

"Marty," she called, poking her head inside. "Can I borrow you for a sec?"

He looked up, startled. "Me? Why do you need me?"

"Well, I know what a whiz you are at robotics and stuff. There's this issue in the auditorium with the big screen that comes down from the ceiling? I thought maybe you could fix it."

Marty raised an eyebrow. "Why would you need the big screen, Emma?"

She hadn't planned on him being so inquisitive—and the clock on the wall read 3:48. Harriet would be waiting!

"Um, I need the screen because I'm doing a big presentation tomorrow," she improvised.

"What's the presentation on?" Marty asked, continuing to fiddle with what looked like a robot body mounted on a board with wheels.

Was he kidding? Couldn't he just come with her

to the auditorium without giving her a pop quiz?

"Well," Marty repeated. "What's it about?"

"If you must know, my advice blog, of course," Emma continued, winging it. "The whole Sadie Hawkins thing has gotten all the girls in seventh grade worried and nervous. So I'm giving a presentation to help them ask boys to the dance."

Marty put down his tools and took off his goggles. "So that's what this is all about," he said, smiling slyly. "You're trying to get me to come with you to the auditorium so you can ask me to the dance. You've got something cool planned, right? Something creative, like you wrote about in your blog post?"

Well, at least someone was paying attention to what she wrote. But that didn't make this any easier—not if he thought it was her who was asking him. "Why would I ask you to the dance?" Emma replied, shaking her head. "That makes no sense, Marty! Harriet likes you and she's my best friend!"

"Aha! So *Harriet* is in the auditorium waiting to ask me to the dance!"

Emma bit her lip. She'd just blown the entire

surprise! She had to cover . . . and quick.

"No, I didn't say that. . . ."

"You didn't have to," Marty said, getting out of his chair and packing up his backpack. "But you kind of gave it away by trying to explain yourself."

Emma didn't know what else to do—so she spilled everything. "Marty, here's the deal: Harriet is going to be totally brokenhearted if I ruin her proposal. So *please* just come with me to the auditorium and act surprised, okay?"

"Okay," Marty said, cheerfully. "You coulda just said that in the first place."

When they reached the auditorium, the doors were unlocked, but everything inside was pitch-black.

"You sure Harriet's in here?" Marty whispered.

"I hope so," Emma said. The way things were going so far, she couldn't be 100 percent sure of anything.

She led Marty to the stage and up the stairs using the flashlight on her phone. "Okay, just hang out here a sec," she announced loudly so everyone would think the plan was working. "I'll try to get the screen down so you can check on why it's sticking."

"Right, why it's *sticking,*" he repeated back to her. "That's why I'm here. To fix the screen. That's the only reason I followed you to the auditorium."

Emma rolled her eyes. Seriously, could he be a worse actor? Harriet would surely sense he had a hunch about their plan if he kept that up!

"Shhh!" she hushed him. Then she shouted, "Okay, Marty! You stand right there and don't move! Be right back!"

With that, a spotlight appeared stage right. Hidden behind the curtain was Harriet, dressed in her makeshift Supergirl costume and Emma's red ladybug galoshes, waiting for her cue.

"I don't have any idea what's going on," Marty said stiffly from center stage. "Not a clue. I'm completely in the dark—literally!"

Harriet looked at Emma, terrified. "OMG! He knows, doesn't he? He guessed! He's so smart!"

"No! Not at all," Emma said, taking her by the shoulders. "Gimme your glasses so they don't fall off when Winston flies you across. You've got this!"

She signaled at Winston and he began to pull Harriet gently up off the ground.

"Not too high!" Harriet begged. When she was about six feet in the air, Winston wrapped the rope around his waist and held it secure. The more he eased up on the tension, the more the harness moved.

"Wave your arms like you're flying!" Emma coached her from the wings. Harriet obeyed, flapping her arms like a bird. She swayed back and forth in the air.

"She doesn't look like Supergirl," Izzy observed. "More like a blue jay in rain boots."

To make matters worse, Harriet was also not flying—more like inching—her way across the stage. "Speed it up a little," Emma called to Winston. "We're going to be here all day."

Winston released the rope a little too quickly and the harness suddenly lurched forward sending a startled Harriet flying toward Marty at full speed. Without her glasses, she couldn't judge exactly how close she was—he looked like a big blur—so she held out her fist and announced, "Here comes Supergirl!"

"I can't look," Izzy said, covering her eyes with her hands. "Tell me when it's over."

Winston tried his best to put the brakes on Harriet, but at the speed she was hurtling toward Marty, he couldn't reel her in. Suddenly, there was a crash.

"Get the lights!" Emma shouted. Winston flipped them on and they all saw what had happened: Marty was lying on his back, holding his nose, and groaning in pain, while Harriet dangled just above him.

"Oh my gosh! She punched him in the face!" Izzy cried.

"Sorry about that," Winston apologized. "I guess the equipment's a little rusty after a year."

"Don't you mean *you're* a bit rusty after a year?" Izzy complained.

Winston lowered Harriet the last few feet down to the stage. "Marty! I'm so sorry!" she said, kneeling at his side. "It was an accident. I'm really nearsighted and I didn't have my glasses on. Or maybe I closed my eyes like Izzy told me? I don't know, but I didn't mean to break your nose!"

Marty sat up. "I don't think it's broken," he said,

wiggling the tip with his fingers. "I think you just knocked the wind out of me."

"I wanted to surprise you," Harriet began to bawl. "And I ruined everything."

Marty took her hand, trying to calm her down. "Well, you certainly surprised me," he said. "And the Supergirl costume was a nice touch."

Harriet peered down at her gymnastics leotard and rain boots. "Really? I don't look silly?"

"You could never look silly," Marty said, blushing. "At least not to me. I think you look great."

"I think you look great," Harriet gushed. "Even if your nose is a little swollen and bleeding." She offered him the edge of her cape to dab it.

Emma breathed a sigh of relief—then stepped up to help her BFF seal the deal. "Harriet has something she wants to ask you, Marty. Don't you, Harriet?"

"Oh, yeah! I almost forgot," Harriet said, shyly. "Marty, it would be *super* if you would go with me to the dance. Get it? Super? Supergirl?"

Marty laughed. "I got it. And yeah, I'd love to go with you."

"Yes!" Emma couldn't help pumping her fist in the air. Her plan hadn't worked perfectly, but it *had* worked.

"Thank goodness," Winston said, mopping the sweat off his forehead with the back of his sleeve. "That was a close one."

"So I don't need to call 911?" Izzy asked everyone.

Emma grinned. "Of course not. Everything is fine. It's more than fine. Harriet has a date for the dance!"

6

DANCE DILEMMAS

Word got around Austen Middle fast—soon everyone knew Harriet and Marty were going to the dance together, and that Emma was partially responsible.

"Your blog is very popular this week," Mr. Goddard told her. He'd seen that her advice inbox was on fire.

"Thanks to the Sadie Hawkins Dance," Emma said. "It's so romantic! The kind of stuff you read about in fairy tales or Jane Austen novels."

Her advisor seemed a little confused by her reaction. "Yes, well, Jane Austen certainly had a tremendous impact on British literature," he replied stiffly.

But love was all Emma could think about. She remembered what her grandma always told her: "There's a lid for every pot." That meant there was someone for everyone out there, someone who was the perfect fit. In her case, she believed it was Jax—at least it had been. She'd felt the connection instantly, from the moment he showed up and took the locker beneath hers. He was the new boy and no one knew anything much about him. But Emma peeled away the layers, one by one. She helped him confide in her and trust her, and he helped her find her voice as a writer. He gave her the confidence to say whatever was on her mind and be her true, authentic self. Someone like that . . . well, he had to be her missing lid, right?

"I think you have your hands full," Mr. Goddard told her. He meant with her blog, not with Jax, but both were true. Instead of going to lunch, Emma nibbled her sandwich in front of a computer station and began responding to her emails.

Dear Emma,

The boy I want to ask to the dance is really into spiders—he has a pet tarantula at home. Any idea how I can ask him in a creative yet creepy, crawly way?

Sincerely,

Sadie Hawkins Stumped

Emma shuddered at the thought of someone actually keeping a huge, hairy spider as a pet! Personally, she preferred puppies, but if that was his passion . . .

She began to type:

Dear Stumped,

Why not decorate his locker with some fake cobwebs and rubber spiders and hang a note from them? Keep your words simple and sincere, something like: "Sorry to bug you . . . but I'd love you to be my date for the dance." I'll leave the puns and prose up to you. Have fun with it and don't stress!

XO,

Emma

Dear Emma,

I asked a boy to the dance and he told me he will "think about it." What does that mean? Is he waiting for someone else to ask him? Is he not sure if he likes me and wants to go with me? Help!

Sincerely,

Utterly Confused

Emma's reply to this one was simple:

Dear Utterly,

I suggest you give this guy a deadline, then move on if he can't stick to it. While he "thinks about it," he's leaving you hanging, which a) isn't very nice and b) isn't very fair. I don't know his reason for not giving you an answer right away, but trust me when I tell you that you deserve one—or at the very least an explanation. This is a good opportunity for you to R-E-S-P-E-C-T yourself and make it clear to that boy that he'd be lucky to go with you. If he's still hesitating, then ask someone else who can make up his mind about how great you are. Hope that helps!

XO,

Emma

As much as she struggled to respond to several emails a day, Emma couldn't keep up with all the Austen girls who wanted her advice.

Saige stopped her in the stairwell. "Do you think I should write Xavier a proposal poem?" she asked Emma.

Emma thought it might be a nice, romantic gesture but wasn't quite sure a seventh-grade boy would appreciate it. "Does he like poetry?"

"Well, I'm not sure. But I'm really good at rhyming. I once figured out a word that rhymed with tangerine."

Emma scratched her head. "Lima bean? Mezzanine? Mr. Clean?"

"Those aren't bad, but mine was better: Frankenstein!"

"I think it's Franken-*stine,*" Emma corrected her. Maybe Saige writing a poem wasn't the best idea?

"I thought I could do it in really pretty calligraphy on parchment paper—something fancy and formal."

Emma sat down on a step—this was going to take a while. "Do you know what you want the theme of the poem to be?" she asked.

"Well, shouldn't it be about Xavier?" Saige replied. "Wait, does anything rhyme with Xavier? Maybe wavier? Gravy-er? Misbehavior?"

"Maybe you should try something more traditional," Emma offered. "Like, 'Roses are red, violets are blue . . .'"

"Xavier, you're awesome—I really like you!" Saige finished her sentence. Then she kept going:

"Your hair is brown,

Your eyes are, too.

If you don't go to the dance with me,

I'll cry boo-hoo!"

"Well, that's a good start," Emma told her. "But maybe it could use a few tweaks here and there . . ."

Undaunted, Saige continued composing her poem:

"When we met at recess, I thought you were cool.

I always smile when I see you in school.

Your braces are metal, your legs are long,

I wrote you this poem instead of a song!"

OMG, Emma thought. There's no stopping her!

"We're having a dance, so ask you I will.

Here goes nothing—it's no fire drill.

If you tell me you'll go, I'll be the happiest girl.

If you tell me you won't, I'll probably hurl."

Emma couldn't take much more. "Saige, I love your spontaneity, but maybe you should slow down a bit?"

"You hate it. You think my poem stinks," Saige said, taking a seat next to her. "It's okay, Emma, you can be honest with me. I asked your advice."

"Well, it's original, that's for sure," she said trying to be gentle. "I just think it could be a little more romantic. Maybe leave out the hurling part."

Saige nodded. "Okay, I can give it another try. But you think I should write him a poem?"

Emma actually didn't hate the idea, even if Saige would never get a job penning greeting cards. "Sure. How could Xavier not appreciate words that come straight from your heart?"

She thought that was the last advice she'd need to give on the spot until Lyla grabbed her just as she was about to walk into the computer lab a few minutes later.

"I'm desperate, Emma," she pleaded. "I need your help."

"Let me guess: You want advice on how to ask a boy to go with you to the Sadie Hawkins Dance?"

Lyla shook her head. "No, it's actually the opposite. I asked a boy and he said yes—but now I'm having second thoughts."

Emma looked puzzled. "I don't get it. You want to take back your proposal?"

"Exactly!" Lyla said. "I thought I wanted to go with Ty Torres but Jordie says no way, he's not cool enough."

Emma knew Ty—he was in show choir with her and played tuba in the Austen marching band. He was also Lyla's next-door neighbor and friend since preschool. Why was Jordie dissing him? Then again, Jordie dissed everyone. . . .

"I think you should do what you want, not what Jordie says," Emma told her. "This isn't cheer squad, it's your personal life."

"I know, I know," Lyla said. "But Jordie says it will be embarrassing for us to double date."

Emma could feel her face start to burn—how dare Jordie judge? "Ty's smart and talented and an amazing rapper," she insisted. "Have you ever heard him do *Hamilton*?"

Lyla nodded. "I have! I'm a total Hamilfan and his parents took us to see the show together on Broadway last summer for my thirteenth birthday. I asked him because I thought it would be fun to hang with him at the dance, but Jordie says none of that matters."

Emma looked Lyla straight in the eye. "Do you really want my advice? Don't dump Ty; he's your friend and it will *crush* him."

Lyla gulped. "Seriously? You think he'll be that hurt?"

"Devastated," Emma insisted. "You can't take back your proposal. Just tell Jordie she has to deal."

"I don't know if I can tell Jordie that," Lyla admitted. "Maybe you could help me convince her that Ty is cooler than she thinks?"

Emma thought for a moment—then remembered the sixth-grade show-choir showcase. The choir had performed "My Shot" from *Hamilton,* with Ty singing the lead.

"Find me at lunch in the cafeteria," Emma instructed her. "We'll put on a little show for Jordie."

#

It took very little convincing to get Ty to agree to rap a *Hamilton* song at seventh-grade lunch—he knew the entire show by heart and loved to perform. Principal Bates, on the other hand, was another story.

"Explain to me again why you and Ty need to cause a disruption during second-period lunch?" she asked Emma.

"It's not a disruption—it's a history lesson," Emma improvised. "About our great country and its founding fathers."

Ty nodded. "Hamilton, Washington, Adams, Jefferson—they're all in the show."

"And why do we need to learn this very important history lesson at this moment?"

Emma knew her principal was suspicious—so she had to come up with a really good answer.

"Well, a lot of kids don't love history class. They think it's boring and they can't relate. We decided we could do something about that."

Principal Bates nodded. "Out of the goodness of

your hearts. This has nothing to do with show choir showing off?"

"Absolutely not!" Emma pretended to be offended. "I was totally inspired by visiting Washington, DC, and looking at the magnificent monuments to our founding fathers. I want to share that with my fellow students."

Ms. Bates raised an eyebrow. "Okay, Emma. I'll let you do it. But I have a hunch you're up to something more."

Emma smiled slyly. "Who? Me? Never!" Then she skipped off with Ty to the cafeteria.

"Okay, you jump up on the table and do your thing," she instructed Ty.

"On the table?" Ty gulped. "In the middle of the entire cafeteria?"

"Yup! We need to make sure Jordie has a front-row seat."

"But what if kids laugh at me?" he considered. "What if they think I'm weird?"

"Been there, done that," Emma assured him. "A

lot of kids made fun of me when I first started writing my blog."

"I remember," Ty said. "Ouch."

"Who cares if they laugh?" Emma said. "You shouldn't. You should never let anyone dull your sparkle!" She pointed to the silver high-top Converse he was wearing. "This is your only shot if you want to go to the dance with Lyla. So get up there, Hamilton, and show 'em what you got."

Inspired, Ty leaped up on the table as Emma hit the Play button on a boom box she'd borrowed from the music room. The *Hamilton* song filled the cafeteria and Ty began to rap: *"I am not throwing away my . . . SHOT!"* The rest of the students—at Emma's urging—gathered around and began clapping along.

"Wow! Everyone says he's as good as Lin-Manuel Miranda," Emma whispered in Jordie's ear.

Jordie spun around, annoyed that her cafeteria clique was being interrupted and she wasn't the one singing a solo. "Really? Who's everyone?"

Emma motioned for Elton and Izzy to back her

up. "I heard some producer saw him and wants him to audition for a role in a Broadway show," Izzy said.

"Oh, yeah. Ty is going to be superfamous," Elton added. "I guess we can say we knew him when."

Now it was Lyla's turn to do some convincing. "He might be even more famous than that girl in our ballet class who did the Kmart commercial in first grade," she told Jordie. "Remember how you invited her to your house every day for a playdate because you thought she'd help you get on TV?"

Jordie twirled her hair. "Broadway, huh?"

Ty suddenly jumped off the table and grabbed a potlid and pan out of the cafeteria lady's hand and started drumming on it. The normally crabby woman smiled and clapped. Then he got down on the floor and started break dancing, spinning on his head like a windmill.

"Woah! Dude can dance!" Elton said, genuinely enthusiastic.

Ty finished his song and the entire cafeteria erupted in thunderous applause. He bowed and signed a few autographs on kids' napkins.

"Fine," she told Lyla. "He can come to the dance with us. Just make sure I get front-row seats when he's on Broadway—and he introduces me to his agent."

Lyla beamed and gave Emma a thumbs-up sign—then she hugged Ty.

That's another one I can check off my list, Emma told herself. Just two more happy people who owe it all to *Ask Emma*!

#

Principal Bates was standing in the back of the cafeteria watching Emma at work.

"That was very impressive," she told her student. "I take it you're trying to help your friends get through their Sadie Hawkins Dance dramas?"

"I may be solving a few problems," Emma admitted. "I'm sorry I couldn't tell you the whole story. I just wanted to help them."

"I understand," Ms. Bates said.

Emma was surprised her principal wasn't sending her straight to detention for lying. "You do?"

Her principal sighed. "'The course of true love never did run smooth.'"

"You can say that again!" Emma took a seat next to her at a cafeteria table.

"I didn't say it. Shakespeare did. But he knew a few things about how difficult it is to find someone you truly care about who feels the same way about you."

Emma assumed she must have been alluding to her on-again, off-again relationship with Jax, until she noticed the sad look on her principal's face.

"Ms. Bates, do you have a date for the Sadie Hawkins Dance?" Emma asked gently.

Ms. Bates chuckled. "Faculty do not bring dates to school dances. We have all of you students and the school to worry about. Trust me, it keeps us all very busy. But thank you for your concern, Emma, and good job today with your 'history lesson.'"

She walked back to her office and Emma couldn't help but feel bad for her. Ms. Bates seemed lonely!

#

"You are *so* not going there!" Izzy insisted when Emma shared what the principal had told her. "Emma, Ms. Bates doesn't need anyone to play Cupid for her!"

They were walking back to Emma's house after school—and Harriet was just as adamant that she abandon the idea immediately.

"Please, no," she begged her. "If she gets mad, she could suspend you, or us, or everyone in seventh grade!"

"I'm not playing Cupid." Emma tried to calm them both down. "I'm just saying that everyone is entitled to find love. And Ms. Bates has no time to look for it, not with all her responsibilities."

"Then that is her problem—not ours," Izzy told her.

"But that's what I do, I solve problems," Emma declared.

"But she didn't ask for your help," Harriet reminded her. "I think you're just avoiding asking Jax to the dance, so you'll do anything to focus on other people's relationships."

"And what's so wrong with that?" Emma responded. "Would you rather I just be a sad, mopey mess? I'm channeling my heartache into something positive. And I think that's a good thing."

"It is," Izzy jumped in, "but Harriet is right. All the other girls asked for your help, Ms. Bates didn't."

"She doesn't need to—I have a sixth sense about people needing assistance," Emma continued, defending her idea. "Think about a time when you felt lonely. What's better than someone caring about you and trying to help?"

"I guess so, but what are you gonna do?" Izzy asked. "It's not like you know a ton of single guys over the age of thirteen."

Izzy did have a point. Who did she know who was middle-aged and looking for a soul mate?

"Is Uncle Billy still single?" she asked her mom when they walked into the kitchen and dropped their school bags on the counter.

"Yes, my younger brother is still single," her mom answered. "He's also off tracking wild antelope in Africa for a National Geographic documentary."

"Ms. Bates wouldn't want a long-distance relationship," Harriet whispered to Emma. "And Africa is really long-distance from Pennsylvania."

"What about the other doctors in Dad's cardiology department at the hospital?" Emma inquired. "Aren't there any heart doctors with lonely hearts?"

Mrs. Woods put down the onion she was dicing for their Taco Tuesday dinner. "And why exactly are you asking about single doctors?"

"It's for Principal Bates," Emma explained.

"Emma, honey, I know you mean well. But you should probably stay out of your principal's personal life."

"That's what I told her!" Izzy exclaimed. "But does she listen to me? Never!"

"Not if there's some way I could help her find someone to take to the Sadie Hawkins Dance," Emma insisted.

"Why don't you google it," Harriet suggested, helping herself to one of Mrs. Woods's oatmeal raisin cookies hot out of the oven. "That's what I do when I need to find something."

"You can't google 'love,'" Emma scolded her. But Harriet cheerfully held up her phone and read out loud: "'Five Ways to Find Real and Lasting Love.'"

Emma snatched the phone out of her hand and read the first bullet point: "'Sometimes love can be right there, right under your nose. Stop and look around you: Is there something or someone you have overlooked in the past?'"

"Harriet, you're a genius!" Emma said, hugging her.

"I am? What did I do?"

"You just gave me a great idea where to find a boyfriend for Ms. Bates. And the article's right—it was under my nose the whole time."

7
DONUT GIVE UP

Every Wednesday, Emma met with Mr. Goddard to discuss her posts and how things were going with her blog. Emma thought he was definite boyfriend material for Ms. Bates! Sure, he was balding and wore bow ties practically every day, but he was also kind and concerned about his students, and he always listened carefully to what they had to say. She was sure that underneath that wrinkled navy cardigan sweater was a big heart just waiting to find its perfect match!

"So it looks like you had about a half-dozen more emails asking about the Sadie Hawkins Dance," he said, looking over her inbox with her. "Do you plan on answering all of these by Friday?"

"I'm organizing them into categories," Emma explained. "So I can answer two or three at a time. Like these three are what I call 'fashion freak-outs.' These students don't know what to wear or if they should dress to impress at the dance. I'm going to give them some style advice."

"I see," Mr. Goddard commented. "And what about this one?"

Emma read the question over carefully. "Oh, that's an easy one. This girl needs a quiet spot to ask a boy to the dance without all his buddies hanging around and listening in. I'm going to tell her to sit under the big oak tree at the edge of the soccer field—that's a nice, quiet, little spot that not a lot of people know about."

"You certainly seem to have things under control," Mr. Goddard said, impressed. "I'm sure your fellow students are very grateful."

"Well, now that you mention it, there is one question that has me a little stumped," Emma said, pulling a piece of paper out of her backpack. "I printed it out to show you. Maybe you have some ideas?"

She handed Mr. Goddard an *Ask Emma* letter she had typed herself—pretending to be in Principal Bates's shoes:

Dear Emma,

I always seem to have so much work to do! I never have time to look for love, because I am up to my ears with my responsibilities. I wish I knew where I could find someone who likes the same things I do: tea, glazed donuts, Shakespeare's sonnets. Do you think there is someone out there looking for love himself?

Signed,

Busy Bee

Emma watched as Mr. Goddard read the note. "So what should I write?" She opened her laptop. "Dear Bee . . ."

"Emma, I don't think this note is from a fellow seventh grader," Mr. Goddard said, slowly. "I think it might be from an adult."

"Really?" Emma pretended to be shocked. "Do you know of an adult who works all the time and likes to drink tea and eat glazed donuts at her desk while reciting Shakespeare?"

Mr. Goddard cleared his throat. "I'm afraid I don't." Emma suspected her advisor knew *exactly* who fit this description but wasn't about to admit it.

"Well, whoever it is seems very interesting," Emma added. "I think I'll go look up some Shakespeare quotes for my response."

She left the computer lab and hid behind the door to the storage closet, waiting to see what Mr. Goddard would do next. Sure enough, he walked out of the room, slicked his hair back with his hand, and headed down the stairs, straight for Ms. Bates's office.

"It's working!" Emma squealed. She ran down the stairs and straight into Jax, who was checking the track-meet schedule on the bulletin board outside of the main office. Great, the last thing she needed was for him to distract her!

"Did Mr. Goddard just go in there?" she asked him.

"Um, yeah, I think so. Why?"

"No reason," Emma fibbed.

Jax watched as she paced back and forth outside the office. "I know there's a reason," he said. "When you're this anxious, there's always a reason."

Emma ignored him and tried to stand still—but her feet had a mind of their own.

"Are you in trouble? Is that why Mr. Goddard went in to talk to Principal Bates?"

Emma scowled. "Seriously? Why do you always assume the worst, Jackson? Why do you always think I'm up to something that will get me in trouble?"

"Um, because I know you, Emma," he replied. "When you have your mind set on how to help someone, you go for it, no matter what the consequences will be."

Emma finally stopped pacing. That sounded strangely like a compliment.

"I'm not in any trouble—not that I know of," she said. "But thanks for worrying about me."

"I wasn't worried," Jax said. "I have other things to do with my time."

Now that sounded like a brush-off!

She had no time to give Jax a piece of her mind—she had to hear what was going on inside Ms. Bates's office. She stood at the door with her ear pressed against it, trying not to look too obvious.

"Is there something you need?" the school receptionist, Ms. Iyala, asked her.

"Nope. Just hangin' out, waiting to ask Mr. Goddard a question. I saw him go in."

She handed Emma a yellow Post-it Note. "I can take a message for you and give it to him."

"It's okay," Emma said. "I don't mind waiting."

Ms. Iyala frowned. "Well, I mind you waiting, Emma. Shouldn't you be in class?"

She did have a point; at this rate, she was going to be super late to English. Luckily, the phone rang and Ms. Iyala was distracted—leaving Emma just enough time to eavesdrop.

"That's very interesting, Judith," she heard Mr. Goddard say. "I had no idea."

Ooh! Maybe Ms. Bates had asked him to the dance! It sounded like he was about to say yes!

"I'll definitely consider it."

Consider what? Was he crazy? He had to think about it? Suddenly, she heard the knob on the door turning. She raced outside and hid behind Jax.

"Emma, what are you doing?" Jax said, trying to step aside.

"Just cover me, will ya?" she said, grabbing his soccer jacket out of his hands and tossing it over her head so Mr. Goddard wouldn't see her as he walked by.

When the coast was clear, she handed him back his bomber. "Not what you had hoped for?" he asked, noting the disappointment on her face.

"No, not exactly," Emma said. But she wasn't about to give up yet. Maybe Ms. Bates and Mr. Goddard didn't know they were perfect for each other. She'd have to give them a nudge.

#

Emma searched the library bookshelves until she found a single leather-bound volume entitled *Shakespeare's Love Sonnets.* She pulled the book down and cracked it open, searching for just the right poem to make her point perfectly. If Ms. Bates loves Shakespeare, then her suitor would have to speak the language.

Finally, her eyes landed on a phrase: "So are you to my thoughts as food to life. . . ." She wasn't quite sure what it meant—but it would be the perfect note to accompany a dozen Yummee Cream Donuts left for Ms. Bates on her desk. How could she resist both Shakespeare *and* donuts?

All she had to do was get to school early, get Ms. Bates out of her office, and sneak in and place the treats where her principal was sure to see them.

"You want us to do *what*?" Harriet put her hands over her ears as Emma explained her plan on the school steps. "No way, Emma. Marty and I are not getting involved in your matchmaking between Mr. Goddard and Ms. Bates!"

"Do I have to remind you that you and Marty are going to the dance together—and that I had something to do with that?"

"Um, you almost broke my nose," Marty chimed in. "I'm not sure I owe you a favor for that."

Harriet patted him on the back. "You tell her, Marty. If Ms. Bates ever catches us breaking into her office, we'll be in deep, deep trouble."

Emma knew she had to appeal to Harriet's love of love. Her BFF was a real softie when it came to romance—she cried every time she watched the Troy and Gabriella karaoke scene in *High School Musical*. "But just picture Ms. Bates's face when she sees this thoughtful, sweet gift on her desk! She'll fall head over heels for Mr. Goddard."

Harriet hesitated; Emma sensed she was about to

cave. "Just think of how happy they'll be—just like you and Marty!" she urged her. "Come on, Harriet. How can you say no to love?"

Harriet looked at Emma, then at Marty, then back at Emma. "Fine. I'll do it."

"Great! We'll do it tomorrow morning. Marty, you tell Ms. Bates you smelled something burning in the school cafeteria and she has to come quick. Harriet, you keep watch while I sneak in and put the donuts on her desk."

"What happens when there's no fire?" Marty asked. "Then what?"

"Then you say, 'Oops! Sorry, I must have been wrong,' and she'll go right back to her office and find a lovely token of affection from her secret admirer."

"Wait, you're not telling her it's from Mr. Goddard?" Harriet asked. "How will she know then?"

"An air of mystery will only add to the romance," Emma explained. "She'll figure it out."

"Or not," Marty said, chuckling. "But at least she'll have a dozen donuts."

They agreed they would get to school at seven sharp—just before Ms. Bates would be arriving and keying into her office.

"As long as everyone sticks to their job, nothing can go wrong," Emma told her BFF and her BFF's BF. Then she thought to herself, *I hope.*

8

TIME TO (WO)MAN UP

Principal Bates was always extremely punctual. She marched into the office at 7:30 a.m. and out at 6 p.m. every single day. Emma, Harriet, and Marty watched and waited for her to walk through the doors of the school lobby, flip on the lights to the main office, and unlock her own inner office. Most of the teachers and staff wouldn't be arriving till eight and that gave them plenty of time to sneak in and out.

"You see? Right on schedule!" Emma said, pushing Marty toward the cafeteria. "Breakfast is served to early-arrival students at seven forty-five, so you go hang out in there for fifteen minutes."

"I wonder if they have French toast," Marty said, scurrying off.

"What do I do?" Harriet asked anxiously.

"You hold the donuts and wait for me to go see if she's in her office," Emma instructed. "I'll signal for you when Marty gets her to leave. And don't squish the donuts! They need to be perfect."

"Yes, ma'am!" Harriet joked and saluted her. "I will guard these donuts with my life."

Emma tiptoed down the hall and poked her head inside the main office. Ms. Bates was in there, all right. Her light was on, and when she pressed her ear to the door, she could make out the clicking of her fingers typing on her keyboard. She ducked in the coat closet, waiting for Marty to come in and do his part.

At exactly 7:45, he walked into the office and knocked on the principal's door.

"Yes?" Ms. Bates asked, opening it.

"Um, come quick, Principal Bates. There's a funny smell in the cafeteria."

Not a funny smell, a burning smell! Couldn't he keep that straight?

"What kind of a smell, Martin?" Ms. Bates asked. "Can you be a little more specific? It might be the egg frittata."

Marty panicked and froze. He couldn't think of what he was supposed to say. Thankfully, Ms. Bates was curious.

"Okay," she told him, "let's go check out this funny smell."

They left the office and Emma jumped into action. "Harriet!" she shouted for her friend down the hallway. "Hurry up!"

Harriet raced down the hall carrying the donuts—then tripped over her shoelace and landed with a *splat* right on them.

"Oh, no!" Emma cried, prying them out from under her. She opened the box to reveal twelve flattened pastries, and the frosting and sprinkles were all stuck to the lid. "They look like pancakes, not donuts!"

"I'm sorry!" Harriet apologized. "It was an accident."

Emma had no choice but to put the slightly mangled box on Ms. Bates's desk along with the note. She was making sure it was right in front of her computer, when she heard footsteps coming.

Oh, no! She's coming back! Emma looked for a place to hide, but there was no time. With nowhere else to go, Emma ducked under the principal's desk. She heard someone enter the room. Her heart felt like it was going to burst out of her chest. What if she got caught? She held her breath as two large feet wearing black sneakers came into view. Emma's brain snapped to attention. Those didn't look like Ms. Bates's feet! Emma had never seen her principal come to school in sneakers. But, before Emma could peek out, the mystery person walked up, dropped something on the desk, and hurried out.

Just as she was pondering, she heard a second set of footsteps coming—this time high-heeled ones! Now those sounded like Ms. Bates's!

The principal walked into her office and stopped in her tracks. She hovered over her desk, and Emma heard her open the box and start munching on a donut.

What if she was trapped here all morning? Where was Harriet when she needed her? She heard another knock on the door and a familiar voice.

"Principal Bates, there's a sink overflowing in the boys' bathroom. You should go see, quick!"

"What is going on in this school today?" Ms. Bates said, frustrated. Her mouth was full of cinnamon cruller. "I haven't been able to sit down at my desk once without being dragged right back out of here!" Emma heard her heels march across the floor.

"Coast is clear," said the voice. "You can come out, now." It was Jax!

He held a hand out to help her up from under the desk.

"Thanks," she said, slightly annoyed that it was him—and not Harriet—who had come to her rescue. "How did you know I was in here?"

"I saw Harriet wipe out on her way down the hall and you run into the office. I figured you were stuck in here, scheming again."

"Is there really a problem with the boys' bathroom?" she asked him.

"Yeah, the sink is running. I turned it on."

Emma laughed—then realized he might get in trouble. "But what if Ms. Bates gets mad that there's no emergency?"

"Well, I had to take that risk to help out a friend, right?"

A friend. So they were back to being friends.

"You didn't have to, but I appreciate it," Emma said—and she meant it.

"So you left Ms. Bates flowers and donuts?" Jax said, checking out the desk.

"Flowers? I didn't leave her flowers." But there they were, a dozen red roses in a vase with a note attached. It read, *That which we call a rose, by any other name, would smell as sweet*, and had no signature.

"I don't believe it!" Emma exclaimed. "Ms. Bates has an *actual* secret admirer!"

#

Emma thought back on the first set of feet she saw when she was hiding in the office. They must have belonged to the secret admirer, because there were no flowers on the desk before he entered the room. Emma only knew a few things about Ms. Bates's potential suitor: He had big feet—about a size 13 like her brother, Luc—and wore black sneakers with bright yellow laces.

"It shouldn't be hard to find the guy," Marty told her. "You just have to check out all the shoes of all the male teachers at Austen."

So that's exactly what she, Harriet, Marty, and Jax did—all day long, they peeked under desks and snooped inside closets. A few had black sneakers, but none with those distinctive neon-yellow laces.

"It's like looking for the princess who fits the glass

slipper," Harriet reflected. "Although it's a prince who fits the running shoe."

"It's more like looking for a needle in a haystack," Marty said. "We have nothing to go on."

But Emma had her hunch. She ran up to the third-floor computer lab—Mr. Goddard was the obvious choice for her principal's secret admirer. She came in the room and saw he was wearing shiny black oxfords similar to the ones her dad wore to work—not running shoes. So it couldn't be him.

"Can I help you, Emma?" he asked.

"I was just wondering how things went with Ms. Bates after our conversation."

Mr. Goddard seemed surprised. "How did you know I spoke with Ms. Bates?"

"Um, just a guess," Emma said, trying to cover. "It wasn't like I saw you go in her office or anything."

Mr. Goddard smiled ever so slightly. "Our talk went just fine, thank you," was all he would share with her. Ugh, fixing up grown-ups was a lot harder than she thought! Why wouldn't they cooperate?

Later in the day, she noticed Ms. Bates walking

down the hall to the library with a smooshed chocolate sprinkle donut in her hand. She couldn't help but stare.

"Is there a problem, Emma?" the principal asked, dabbing at her lips with a napkin.

"Nope, no problem." Emma tried to smile and look innocent. The last thing she needed was for Ms. Bates to suspect her of the donut delivery!

At the end of the day, Emma had practically given up on finding the mystery man who had left flowers—until she saw Mr. Goddard leaving school in a running jacket and sweatpants. There, on his feet, were the black sneakers with neon-yellow laces!

"You!" Emma couldn't help blurting out. "Those are your sneakers!"

Mr. Goddard looked down at his feet. "Yes, I power walk to and from work. It's how I squeeze exercise into my workday."

Emma didn't know what else to say—she couldn't tell him she knew he was Ms. Bates's secret admirer. She couldn't admit that she had been hiding under the desk and saw him.

"Well, they're very nice sneakers," she said, thinking quickly. "I might get my dad ones just like it for his birthday."

Mr. Goddard nodded. "Well, they're quite comfortable—and they're on sale at Sports-R-Us." He took off down the street, leaving Emma standing outside the school.

"Do I have you to thank for my flowers and donuts?" Ms. Bates said, sneaking up behind her.

"What? Huh? N-n-n-no," Emma stuttered.

"Really?" Ms. Bates pressed her. "You didn't put the idea into . . . anyone's head?"

Emma felt her face flush. "Well, I might have mentioned something. . . ."

"I thought so," Ms. Bates said. "Have a good evening, Emma."

Emma had to ask—she needed to know! "So do you know who your secret admirer is?"

"I do. He told me just before he left. He didn't want to keep me in suspense."

And?! Emma searched her principal's face for a

clue: Did this mean she and Mr. Goddard were now a couple?

"If you're wondering, Mr. Goddard will help me chaperone the Sadie Hawkins Dance. But it's not a date—it's two colleagues going together, just keeping each other company."

"That's great, Ms. Bates!" Emma said. "I'm so happy for you."

"You know what, Emma? I'm happy, too. It will be nice to have someone to talk to."

Ms. Bates said she was happy, and that was all Emma ever wanted to accomplish—even if it meant destroying a dozen donuts in the process.

9

ON YOUR MARK . . . GET SET . . . PROPOSAL!

After she knew that Jordie was no longer a threat, Izzy decided she simply would not worry about asking Elton to be her date for the dance. She would take her time and calm her nerves before she asked him. But Emma was anxious to get her other BFF set. She hated leaving loose ends untied! Mr. Goddard and Ms. Bates were paired up, and Marty and Harriet looked so happy feeding each other french fries at the cafeteria table. She wanted Izzy to have the same joy in her life. Even if Izzy could wait patiently, she couldn't!

"Aren't they the cutest?" Emma asked, watching Marty wipe ketchup off Harriet's cheek with a napkin. *"#relationshipgoals."*

"Yuck!" Izzy said, turning around to see what she was mooning over. "I hate mushy couples."

"Speaking of which . . ." Emma began, grateful her friend had brought up the topic. "How are we going to make Elton and you a couple?"

"*We* are not going to do anything. *I* am going to ask him . . . when I'm good and ready. I know you like to help, Emma, but trust me, I've got this."

Emma frowned. Why did Izzy have to be so stubborn? Couldn't she see Emma was on a roll? She had to convince her to take action before it was too late. What if Elton said yes to someone else?

"You know, I heard Elton telling some boys by the water fountain he wasn't going to the dance *at all,"* she casually told her friend.

Izzy stopped sipping her container of chocolate milk. "He said that? Well, what does he know?"

"He *doesn't* know you're planning on asking him—so we better get to it!" Emma prodded her.

"Ugh, there goes that *we* again!"

Emma opened her binder where she had scribbled down an entire page of notes titled "Operation Elton." She took out a pen and highlighted a few key points and began reading them to Izzy. "I was thinking you should ask him in a sporty way—something that speaks to him and is also so *you*."

Izzy looked puzzled. "What do you want me to do? Put it up on the big scoreboard: 'Elton, will you go with me?'"

"That's not a bad idea." Emma jotted some more notes in her book. "Maybe during one of his soccer games?"

"No way," Izzy said. "No one is allowed to touch the scoreboard, especially when there's a game in play."

"Elton loves to win, doesn't he?" Emma continued thinking out loud.

"Well, of course. Every athlete wants to win,"

Izzy said. "I hate it when I lose one of my gymnastic meets."

"Then that's it! You let him win. Challenge him to a race and when he crosses the finish line first, Harriet and I will be there waiting for him, holding a poster that says, 'How's this for a winning idea: Go with Izzy to the dance!'"

Izzy stared. "You mean you want me to not do my best in a competition? You want me to purposely lose?"

Emma shrugged. "You say that like it's a bad thing."

"It is!" Izzy insisted. "It's not what athletes do."

"Well, could ya do it just this once? If it makes Elton say yes to going to the dance with you?"

Izzy considered. "I dunno, Emma. It just doesn't feel . . . right."

"That's because you're thinking it's a real race. It's not. It's just part of the plan. And it's a brilliant plan, if I do say so myself. You just have to make Elton want to race you."

"Well, that's easy," Izzy assured her. "His ego is bigger than a soccer field."

Emma put an arm around Izzy. "I know you can do this, Iz. And don't think of it as losing a competition. Think of it as winning a date!"

"I guess," Izzy said, still hesitant. "If you think it'll work."

"Think?" Emma replied. "I know it will, one hundred percent!"

#

Emma made sure she and Izzy waited for the same school bus as Elton after school. They stood right behind him in line, talking loudly, so he could hear every word they were saying. If his ego was as big as Izzy had said, he was going to jump right in with his opinion. . . .

"I can't believe how fast you ran the track in gym class, Iz," Emma began their staged conversation. "I'd hate to challenge you to a race."

"I'd hate to challenge me, too," Izzy boasted. "My feet were literally lightning! I'm sure I have the fastest track time in all of Austen Middle."

Elton turned around to interrupt. "The fastest time? Yeah, right. Just stick to your balance beam and somersaults, Iz. I've been running track since fifth grade, and no one comes close to my time."

The corners of Izzy's mouth began to twitch. She hadn't wanted to fake this race, but Elton was insulting her athletic ability—and no one did that without a fight. "Oh yeah? Wanna bet?" she taunted him.

"I mean, a gymnast isn't a track-team captain," Elton continued. "I'm sure you're really fast and all, but not as fast as me."

"I can totally beat you in a race," Izzy countered. "Without breaking a sweat. And the loser has to buy the winner a Super Quadruple Scooper Sundae at Freddy's."

Elton's mouth was practically watering. "Twice around the track. The slowest runner buys." They shook hands on it.

"So how about tomorrow? During recess?" Emma suggested. "I'm happy to be an impartial judge at the finish line."

Elton smiled. "This is too easy. I almost feel bad. But I'll ask a friend to be a judge, too—just to make sure no one cheats."

Izzy pointed a finger in his face. "Hah, as if I'd ever cheat! I don't need to. I'm going to leave you in my dust."

"Better start counting your piggy-bank money to pay for my sundae!" he fired back.

"Don't underestimate girl power," Izzy countered.

Emma noticed how their faces were only inches apart as they bantered back and forth. It was so romantic! And Izzy was right; Elton couldn't resist a challenge. Wait till he crossed that finish line and saw what was waiting for him!

#

Izzy wasn't the slightest bit worried about the race—but Harriet was a nervous wreck!

"Do you think I put enough glitter on the poster?" she asked her two friends, dragging it with her as they made their way onto the field. "Maybe I should have made the letters bigger?"

"Trust me, they're big enough," Izzy assured her. "He'll be able to read it from way back on the track."

"But we don't *want* him to see it," Emma reminded them. "Not till the moment he crosses the finish line. That's when we do the big reveal."

"What do we say?" Harriet asked. "Congrats! You win a date with Izzy?"

Emma giggled. "We hold up the sign and let him read it. Then, Izzy, you step forward and say, 'Surprise!'"

Izzy was too busy stretching to pay attention. "Remember," Emma told her. "You start running fast, then slow down and let Elton get way out in front of you."

"Well, maybe not *that* far in front," Izzy said. "I think a few feet is plenty. I don't want this to go to his head."

Emma rested a hand on her shoulder. "Iz, we're doing this for Elton, remember? He needs to be excited and happy that he won."

"Fine, fine," Izzy agreed. "I'll go slower . . .

eventually. After I let him see how wrong he was."

"You could even trip—or bend down to tie your shoelace," Emma suggested. "Anything that doesn't look too obvious that you're letting him go ahead of you."

"Gee, maybe I could kick my sneaker off and run back to get it?" Izzy said, becoming annoyed.

"Ooh, that's good," Harriet said, approvingly. "Elton would never suspect that."

Just then, Elton strode onto the field—with Jax by his side.

"Uh-oh," Emma muttered under her breath. Things between them were definitely improving, but they hadn't completely made up yet.

"What's he doing here?" Harriet asked.

Looking at me with those deep blue eyes, Emma thought.

"Hey," Jax said simply, walking over to them. "Elton asked me to watch the race."

"To make sure no one cheats," Elton said, pointing at Izzy.

"How would I do that?" Izzy asked. "Put wheels on my sneakers?"

"Ya never know," Elton answered. "You girls are tricky."

She held up her foot. "See? Just an ordinary pair of Nikes."

"I'll just stand back here." Jax motioned to where Harriet was waiting with the poster behind her back.

"No!" Emma said, worried he'd discover their plan and give it away. "Stand with me. Right here by my side."

She noticed that Jax blushed ever so slightly at her suggestion. "Oh, okay," he said.

"So you get a good view of the race," Emma added—just in case he was getting any ideas that she had forgiven him. She didn't mind feeling his arm brush against her, but she had to make sure everything went perfectly for Izzy and Elton.

"You'll go all the way down there and take your places at the starting line," Emma explained to the runners as she pointed to the opposite side of the field.

"Then I'll blow the whistle and you'll start running as fast as you can around the track."

"'As fast as you can,'" Elton echoed her. "Got that, Izzy? Because it's not gonna be as fast as me."

Izzy rolled her eyes. She was used to opposing teams trying to psych her out before a competition. "Whatever you say. Lemme know if you want me to give you a five-minute head start—'cause you'll need it." Izzy marched toward the starting line. "I'm ready," she said. Elton quickly stopped stretching and ran to catch up to her.

"Those two," Emma said, shaking her head. "They're so cute."

"Cute?" Jax suddenly piped up. Oops, she had forgotten he was standing right there. "I think they hate each other."

"Hate each other? Can't you see they're meant for each other?" Emma protested. "Honestly, Jax, how can you not see it?"

"It sounded like they were fighting to me."

"Well, sometimes couples fight. It doesn't mean

they hate each other," Emma insisted.

"Really? So if they fight, they actually *like* each other?" He winked.

Ugh, Emma thought, why did he have to flirt with her?

"Okay, they're in their places," she changed the subject abruptly. She waved down the field and held her whistle in the air.

"Do you want a countdown or something?" Jax asked. "Like, on your mark, get set, go?"

Emma hadn't actually thought about that but it sounded like a good idea. "Sure. Go for it."

He cleared his voice. "On your mark!" he shouted as Izzy and Elton readied their stances. "Get set! GO!"

Emma blew the whistle and watched as her BFF and Elton began to bolt around the track.

"Wow, Izzy is pretty fast," Jax noted. "She's keeping up with Elton."

That's what you think, Emma chuckled to herself.

"They're halfway around the first lap," Jax commented. "And they're neck and neck."

Come on, Iz, slow down, Emma silently willed

her. Stumble, trip, fall . . . anything! Just let Elton take the lead. Instead, Izzy began to speed up even more.

"She should join the Austen track team," Jax said, amazed. "She's really fast."

Emma glanced back over her shoulder at Harriet who looked as concerned as she was. She motioned for her to step forward to the finish line.

"What do we do now?" Harriet whispered to her.

"Pray," Emma said.

Thankfully, Jax was now coaching Elton to pick up the pace. "Come on, Elton! Take it home! You got this!"

I hope he's got this, Emma thought. If not, Izzy is going to be dateless for the dance!

Jax continued jumping up and down and waving Elton toward the finish line. But his cheering only seemed to make Izzy more determined to outrun her opponent. She pushed herself even harder as she came around the track for the second time.

"She isn't slowing down," Harriet said, tugging on Emma's sleeve. "What if she wins?"

Emma hadn't considered that possibility. She had gone over the plan with Izzy a dozen times and she knew what she had to do. But, when her friend got into competitive mode, there was nothing—and no one—that could stop her.

As Emma watched, Izzy pulled in front of Elton and headed for the homestretch.

"I don't believe this!" Jax exclaimed.

"Neither do I," Emma said, shaking her head.

As Izzy made her way toward the finish line, Elton was at least a full ten feet behind her. She crossed the line, waving her hands in the air.

"I won! I did it! I beat the fastest boy on the track team!" she shouted. "I am the champion!"

Emma crossed her arms over her chest. "Seriously, Iz? Could you not pay attention to *any* part of the plan?"

Jax raised an eyebrow. "Plan? What plan?" Just then Elton crossed the finish line, huffing and puffing.

"I won! I won!" Izzy bragged.

Emma elbowed Izzy sharply in the ribs. "Izzy, you are killing any chance of this working."

"Wait, what is supposed to be working?" Jax repeated himself. "And what is this plan?"

Emma gave Harriet a little shove. "Show Elton the poster."

"I can't," Harriet said, keeping it hidden behind her back. "It says, 'How's this for a winning idea?' and he clearly lost."

"Oh, gimme that," Izzy said, grabbing the poster out of her hands. She held it up. "Elton, do you wanna go to the dance with me or not?"

Elton was still trying to catch his breath—so Jax spoke for him. "Hold on a second: Izzy was supposed to lose? *That* was your plan? To throw the race?"

Emma shuffled her feet on the track. "Kinda. Maybe."

"But why?" Jax was absolutely outraged. "Why would you ever tell Izzy to do that?"

"So Elton would like her and say yes," Harriet tried to explain.

Elton held up his hand. "Can I say something?"

"Please," Emma replied. "Anything." She was getting tired of Jax scolding her.

"Yes. I say yes." Elton took Izzy's hand.

For the first time Emma could remember, she saw Izzy blush. "Really? You'll go to the dance with me? Even after I kicked your butt?"

"Of course! You're competitive and never pull your punches. You drive me crazy, and that's what I love about you. I haven't had to run that hard all year. I liked it. But I have one condition."

"Oh, and what's that?" Izzy smirked.

"In the tradition of Sadie Hawkins, you pay for the sundaes."

Izzy handed off the poster to Harriet with her free hand. "Deal," she said, hugging Elton. They walked off the field together, talking and laughing.

"Wow," Emma said, breathing a sigh of relief. "That went surprisingly well. Chalk up another couple going happily ever after to the Sadie Hawkins Dance."

"Emma, sometimes you go too far," Jax corrected her. "Izzy didn't need some crazy scheme to get Elton to say yes. She could have just asked him."

"But I used all this glitter," Harriet said, looking

down at her sign. "It would have gone to waste."

"I'm just saying that sometimes you think too much, Emma, and you get carried away. Izzy didn't have to throw the race to get Elton to go with her. She just needed to be herself."

Emma considered what he was saying: It *was* her BFF's competitive spirit and drive that made her so special. And Izzy had handled the situation just fine on her own; maybe she didn't need to scheme after all? Maybe Jax was right?

"So you think I'm a horrible person?" she asked him. "For telling Izzy to pretend to be someone she wasn't."

Jax looked deep into her eyes. "No, I know you mean well, Emma. But sometimes you make things more complicated than they need to be. You know?"

Know *what*? Was he hinting that she should just ask him to the Sadie Hawkins Dance, right then and there? Was he trying to tell her he would say yes?

"We're gonna be late for next period," Harriet said, tugging on her sleeve. "Let's go, Em."

Emma jogged along with Harriet, leaving Jax trailing behind them. Still, she couldn't help thinking about what he had just told her. Was all her plotting really unnecessary? Did she go too far? Then she remembered: Thanks to her advice, everyone was coupling up!

Everyone, except her and Jax . . .

10 PRINCE CHARMING

That night, Emma had a dream: In it, she was climbing to the top of the Washington Monument, trying to reach Jax, who was seated at the tippy top, hovering above it on a cloud. Winston was holding a rope and pulling her up slowly on the Peter Pan harness.

"You'll never make it," Jax taunted her from his seat. "You always get carried away and make things more complicated than they need to be, Emma."

Emma ignored him and continued scaling the monument, trying not to look down at the ground disappearing beneath her. Just as she got a few inches from Jax, Winston lost his grip and the rope slipped. He tried his best but couldn't stop it. She felt herself tumbling down, down, down. . . .

"Help! I'm falling!" she screamed.

She suddenly felt her mom gently shaking her awake. "Emma, honey, it was just a bad dream. You're okay."

"But it seemed so real," Emma said, blinking her eyes open.

"Do you want to tell me about it?" her mom asked, tenderly stroking her hair and wiping away her tears.

"Mom, how did you get Dad to date you?"

Her mother hesitated, slightly embarrassed by the question. "Emma, it was more than twenty years ago."

"Please, Mom!"

Mrs. Woods sat down on the edge of the bed. "Actually, he asked *me* out. I never thought I would be interested in dating a premed student—they all seemed so serious. But he changed my mind."

"So what did he do to convince you?"

Her mom thought for a moment. "It's not really *what* he did, but how he did it. He was very persistent."

Emma sat up straight in her bed—so that was where she got her determination from! "Tell me more," she pleaded.

"The first time we met, we were walking in opposite directions across the quad. I was wearing this red sundress with black polka dots that I loved. He stopped me and told me I looked like a watermelon—which I didn't find funny at all. But he asked one of my friends my name and my dorm, and then he showed up the next day to apologize holding a giant watermelon with a bow on it."

Emma giggled. "That is pretty funny. Most guys would bring flowers or chocolates."

"Your dad never did anything most guys did. He once took me on a date to a supermarket."

"A supermarket? Why?" Emma asked, drying her tears.

"We were having this debate over which cereal was better, Lucky Charms or Rice Krispies."

"Lucky Charms of course!" Emma said. "All those yummy little marshmallows."

"That's what your father thought, but I liked how Rice Krispies always snapped, crackled, and popped when you poured milk on them. So he took me grocery shopping to buy both. Then we had a taste test."

"Was he right?"

"Well, Lucky Charms became my favorite cereal," Mrs. Woods admitted. "And your dad became my boyfriend."

"So you're saying that it was Dad's sense of fun that made you fall for him?" Emma asked.

"That was part of it, for sure," her mom replied. "I guess what I loved is how he always spoke his mind and his heart. He never tried too hard to impress me. He was just, well, your dad, and one of the realest boys I'd ever met."

Emma considered. "So, if he had come right out and asked you to, oh, I don't know, go with him to a school dance, you would have said yes?"

"Once I got to know him, I knew he was the one for me. So yes, I would have gone with him to every dance—which I did. And I would have married him—which I also did."

"Did you have a fancy proposal? A poster with glitter?"

Mrs. Woods laughed. "Emma, your father proposed to me over a bowl of Lucky Charms! He hid the ring in the cereal—I could have swallowed it. But it was sweet and simple and very us. It was all I needed to know I wanted to be Mrs. Peter Woods."

Emma nodded. So maybe Jax *was* right. Maybe she had gone too far by advising Harriet to dress up like Supergirl and Izzy to fake losing the race. Maybe Jax didn't need or want all of that. Maybe all she had to do was just go up to him and say the words. . . .

"Try and get some sleep," her mom said, tucking her in. "No more nightmares. Just sweet dreams sprinkled with Lucky Charms marshmallows."

Emma yawned. If it worked for her mom and dad all those years ago, could it work for her and Jax, too?

#

Emma arrived at school extra early the next morning—she wanted to be at the lockers before Jax arrived, calm, collected, and ready to ask him to the dance. But, as soon as she saw him walking down the hallway toward her, her heart began to pound and her palms got all sweaty.

"Hey, Jax," she said meekly.

"Hey, Emma," he replied. "Something I can help you with?"

"Actually, you already did." She took a deep breath. "You know how yesterday you told me that sometimes I get carried away and complicate things? Well, you were right. So I'm just gonna keep this short, sweet, and to the point: Jax, will you go to the Sadie Hawkins Dance with me?"

There was a long silence as Jax stood there looking stunned.

"Um, hello?" Emma hadn't expected *this* reaction. He was completely speechless. "Did you hear what I just said? I asked you to the dance with me."

"I know, I know," Jax said, brushing the hair out of his eyes. He didn't look excited or happy; in fact, the color had drained from his face completely. "Emma, I would have loved to have gone with you. But someone already asked me yesterday after school—and I said yes. I'm so sorry!"

Emma didn't know whether to scream or burst into tears. "What? How could you?"

"Well, you didn't seem interested in asking me. You were helping everybody else with their proposals, and you have hardly even talked to me since our argument. I figured I was the last person you wanted to go with."

"Jax, it was so obvious I wanted to ask you!"

"Really?" Now he sounded hurt. "You wrote in your blog how you felt about me for everyone to read. You made me sound like a real jerk."

Emma vaguely recalled the first post she wrote at the start of all the Sadie Hawkins hysteria: *"If a boy were going to reject me, I would hope he would do it politely and compassionately, not simply ice me out of his life with little or no explanation."*

"Well, you did ice me out. You were really cold after we got back from DC," she tried to defend herself.

"I was really stressed with schoolwork, and okay, maybe a little scared to go out with you."

"Why?" Emma cried. "Why would you be scared of me?"

"Because sometimes you're a little intense, Emma. You're really smart and clever, and despite the obstacles, you always make good things happen. But I don't know if I can keep up with you. Sometimes I feel like you want me to be someone perfect, and I don't know if you actually like me for me."

Emma's scowl softened. "Jax, I think you're awesome, too. And we don't have to keep up with each other. We kinda make each other better."

Then she remembered he had said no—and disappointment washed over her. "Why couldn't you wait till I asked you?"

"The dance is only a week away, and Jordie asked really nicely. She gave me a dozen roses and everything."

Emma gasped. "Jordie? You're going with Jordie?" Of all the girls at Austen it had to be her?

"Emma, I would much rather go with you, but I can't take it back and hurt Jordie's feelings. That would be really mean."

Jax was right—he couldn't do that. Which is why she needed to come up with a scheme, just one more time, to find Jordie her perfect date for the dance.

"I know I said I was done fibbing and plotting," she began. "But it's the only way to get Jordie to un-ask you to the dance so we can go together."

Jax raised an eyebrow. "And how exactly do we get her to do that?"

Emma was stumped. How could she get Jordie to change her mind about Jax in a way that wouldn't hurt anyone's feelings. "I've got it!" Emma grinned. "Whenever our dog, Jagger, steals something out of the trash can, the only way to get him to drop it is to dangle something better in front of his nose. Like a treat or a toy."

"Wait, am I a piece of garbage in this analogy?" Jax asked, laughing.

"You're missing the point! We just need to dangle something better in front of her. Someone Jordie likes more." Then again, there weren't many boys at Austen who made Jordie's heart do backflips. "I don't suppose you have Noah Centineo's email?" she asked Jax.

Jax rolled his eyes.

"Okay," Emma said. "I'll just have to find someone that Jordie doesn't know she likes yet who likes her."

Suddenly, Winston walked by, avoiding her gaze. She knew the whole Harriet falling-from-the-sky fiasco had probably scared him off. But maybe, just maybe . . . Emma took a good hard look at him: He did have nice green eyes under those Harry Potter glasses. And if he actually brushed his hair and tucked in his shirt, he was kinda cute.

"Winston," Emma began. "Can I talk to you a sec?"

Winston gulped. "Oh, no. I am not rigging up the harness and flying someone over the stage again. I can't, Emma. That was an epic fail."

"Forget about the flying," she said, smiling sweetly. "I just need you to help me find some old videos of *Peter Pan* from sixth grade—and maybe arrange a private screening in the auditorium. Leave everything else to me."

It was that last part that Winston hated—it meant he was in for more than he bargained for. "Emma, not again . . ."

Emma remembered a Shakespeare quote she had stumbled upon when searching for one for Ms. Bates's secret admirer note. She recited to both boys:

"'It is not in our stars to hold our destiny, but in ourselves.'"

Winston scratched his head. "What the heck does that mean?"

Emma grinned. "Trust me!"

11

STAGING THE PERFECT PROPOSAL

Emma knew that if she was going to make this work, it would take a village—or at least an entire show choir. She recruited several members of their club and asked them for a favor—a big favor—all in the name of romance. With the proper mood and setting, she would then dangle the treat under Jordie's nose. Lyla agreed to help her (since she had saved her from having to dump Ty), and they figured out that the lockers before gym class would be the best place for them to corner Jordie.

"So, do you think you'll star in the seventh-grade musical this year?" Lyla asked Jordie as they got ready for PE class.

"Of course!" she replied with a wave of her hand. "Once a star, always a star."

Emma craned her head around the corner of the lockers. It wouldn't be easy to play into Jordie's ego, but she had to do it for her and Jax! "So I hear Ms. Otto is planning on doing *Cinderella,*" she informed them. "Winston told me."

"Winston? How would he know?" Jordie said dismissively.

"Oh, he knows," Lyla jumped in. "He always knows everything going on behind the scenes."

"He told me that he told Ms. Otto he couldn't think of anyone more perfect than you to play a princess," Emma added.

Jordie stopped fixing her hair in the mirror. "He said that? About me?"

"He said no one else could even come close to topping you as Peter Pan last year. And he should know! He was the one who kept the spotlight on you the whole show."

It was Lyla's turn next: "Aw, that's so sweet! Don't you think, Jordie?"

Jordie mulled it over. "Winston? Sweet? I guess I never thought about it."

"A boy like that is hard to find," Emma added. "Someone who thinks you're beautiful and talented."

Jordie's cheeks flushed. "He said I was talented? And beautiful?"

"He's such a romantic!" Emma said, sighing. "I'm sure the girl he goes with to the dance is going to be showered in gifts and flowers."

Jordie suddenly snapped out of her trance. "Girl? What girl?"

"Oh, I can't say," Emma continued. "As an advice blogger, I have to protect my client's privacy." She remembered her dad once telling her about the oath doctors take. What was it? "I can never break my

Hypocritical Oath. I think that's what it's called. . . ."

"If you know who is asking Winston, you have to tell me," Jordie said, shaking her.

"But why? Don't you already have a date to the dance?" Lyla pointed out. "Aren't you going with Jax?"

"*You're* going with Jax?" Emma pretended to be surprised. "Wow. Good luck with that."

"What do you mean? You like him," Jordie said. "Everyone knows that."

"Well, maybe I *liked* him when were on the Student Congress together. But that was before he told me I couldn't order my favorite flavor of ice cream at Freddy's. He always wants everything his way, and I don't want to date a boy who bosses me around." She didn't like having to make things up about Jax, but she didn't see any other options. Jordie had to see that Winston was a better choice.

"Wait!" Jordie cried. "I changed my mind. I don't want to go with Jax to the dance."

Emma tried hard not to laugh. "Really? Are you

sure about that, Jordie? It might hurt Jax's feelings."

"Too bad! I am not going with a boy who's bossy! I'll ask Winston and of course he'll say yes." She snapped her fingers at Emma and Lyla. "Make it happen. Today." She slammed her locker shut and stormed off into the gym.

"Whatever you say, Jordie," Lyla called after her.

"Get her to the auditorium right after the last-period bell rings," Emma instructed her. "I'll do the rest."

#

Winston had no idea what Emma had up her sleeve. All he knew was that she wanted the huge projection screen set up and ready to go with video highlights from *Peter Pan*. Now that the last period was over, she had to convince him that Jordie was the girl of his dreams—and she had about ten minutes to do it!

"Wasn't Jordie amazing as Peter Pan?" she asked

him as they fast-forwarded through the clips.

Winston blushed. "Well, yeah. I mean, Jordie is amazing in every show she does."

"She told me she was so grateful for all you did for the production. She loved your lighting design."

Winston pushed his glasses off the tip of his nose. "She did? She said that?"

"And she told me she felt so safe flying onstage, knowing you had her back."

Winston gasped. "Seriously? She noticed me?"

"Noticed you? How could someone *not* notice you, Winston? You're a really nice person, and you hold the whole show together!"

Winston's eyes lit up. "Do you think Jordie thinks that? About *me*?"

Emma was trying her best not to embellish things too much—Jax had made her see the error of her past ways. "I think she could. If she opened her eyes and saw who you really are."

Winston sighed. "No girl has ever liked me before."

Emma glanced at the clock on the wall. "Winston, I need you to do me a little favor. Actually, it's a favor for Jordie. In about five minutes, she's coming in here to ask you to go with her to the Sadie Hawkins Dance."

Winston suddenly looked confused—and terrified. "What? What do I do? Where do I go?"

She escorted him to the center of the stage. "You just pretend you have no idea what I just told you and I'll run the video. Let Jordie do all the talking and you act surprised."

"Surprised? I'm shocked!" Winston cried. "And I don't like to be the center of attention. That's why I'm always behind the scenes."

"Well, that's great," Emma improvised. "Because Jordie loves to be in the spotlight. You stay right there and let her run the show."

He had no time to argue—the choir began to file in and take their places onstage behind him.

"What's going on here, Emma?" Winston whined. "I don't like this!"

Next came Lyla leading Jordie down the aisle to the stage. And Emma noticed Jax sneaking in and taking a seat in the very back of the auditorium to watch her plan unfold.

Emma signaled the choir to start singing: *"It's not on any chart / You must find it with you heart / Never Neverland . . ."*

"Listen," Emma cooed in Jordie's ear. "We got the choir to sing your song and set the mood."

She then started the video on the screen: Jordie appeared on it, larger than life, in her Peter Pan costume. She was so mesmerized by her own image, Emma had to gently nudge her and remind her why she was there.

"Um, Jordie? You wanted us to get Winston here. Remember?"

"Huh? Oh, yeah," Jordie said. "I was really good as Peter Pan, wasn't I?"

Emma looked over at Winston and signaled for him to step forward and speak up.

"Um, you were great," he told Jordie, shyly. "A real star."

Jordie was about to fire off a quick proposal—but paused. "You think I'm a star?"

"Um, yes?" Winston replied.

Jordie actually looked touched—or maybe just a tiny bit smitten?

"Now would be a really good time to ask something," Emma prodded her.

Jordie looked around at the stage full of singers and Lyla and Jax looking on. "I do—but I think I want to do it alone. Show's over—everyone out!"

Winston nodded. "Okay, I'll go then."

"Wait! No!" Jordie said, taking him by the hand. "Not you. You stay."

Emma hid behind the stage curtain, listening to the conversation unfold.

"So," Jordie began, "Winston . . ."

"That's my name."

Jordie frowned. "It's a nice name, I guess. Maybe a little stuffy. Has anyone ever called you Winnie?"

"Like Winnie the Pooh?" Winston replied. "Uh, no, not really."

"Good! Then, I will! Winnie, do you want to go

with me to the Sadie Hawkins Dance?"

Winston nodded again. "Um, yes."

She breathed a huge sigh of relief. "Okay, good! I'll email you the details of what you should wear and what gifts you should bring me on the night of the dance." She paused a second and added quietly, "And thanks, by the way, for telling Ms. Otto I would make the perfect princess. That was sweet."

Winston smiled nervously—he had no idea what she was talking about, but Jordie had just thanked him and told him he was sweet. "Oh, you're welcome."

Jordie quickly exited the auditorium just as Jax ducked down behind a seat so she wouldn't spot him still there.

Emma popped out from behind the curtain. "What just happened?" Winston asked her in disbelief.

"I got you a date for the dance with Jordie—and you're gonna have an amazing time, Winnie the Pooh Bear!" Emma told him.

Winston couldn't stop smiling. "I'm going to the dance. With Jordie! Wow!"

Jax raced down the aisle to the stage. "Emma, you did it! You actually did it. That was incredible."

It *was* pretty incredible, if she did say so herself. Things were actually going perfectly! Now, she had the dance in a week to look forward to—with Jax as her date.

12

THE PERFECT STORM

The weatherman called it “a record-breaking nor’easter”—the most rainfall and the strongest winds New Hope, Pennsylvania, had ever seen. All the storm radars indicated it would make landfall on Thursday night—the night of the Sadie Hawkins Dance.

Principal Bates watched the weather report all day before making her final decision. “I’m afraid we will have to postpone the seventh-grade dance," Principal Bates informed the students over the loudspeaker Thursday afternoon. Everyone please stay safe and dry tonight. Once the storm passes, we'll be able to reschedule."

Everyone was disappointed, but no one more than Emma. She had worked so hard to make matches and counsel her peers ensuring a perfect evening. Now, everything was ruined, just ruined. There would be no dance, no beautiful pink decorations, no confetti cannon, and worst of all, no Jax.

She listened in bed that night as the rain beat forcefully against the windows and the wind whipped through the trees of their backyard. The lights flickered on and off, and her mom and dad made sure that she and Luc each had a flashlight in case they lost power altogether. When she awoke in the morning, there were downed power lines and uprooted trees everywhere. "School is canceled for today," her mom came in to inform her. Luc was cheering from his room—his high school had also closed. "Thankfully the school didn't lose electricity, but Ms. Bates says the gym is totally flooded and they need to get the water pumped out."

"Flooded?" Emma gasped. "Where are we supposed to have the Sadie Hawkins Dance?"

"I think that's the last thing on Principal Bates's mind," her dad told her. "The entire basement level of Austen Middle is underwater. It'll be a long time before that gym is ready to be used."

Emma couldn't believe it. It wasn't bad enough that the dance was canceled yesterday, now it would never happen? She looked at her dress hanging from a hook on her closet door. It was a beautiful shade of purple crushed velvet, with a wrap front and ruffles along the hemline. When she saw it in the window of Daniella's Dress Boutique, she knew it was the one. She had been counting the hours till the dance—and *this* had to happen.

"It's a natural disaster," her father tried to soothe her frazzled nerves. He was watching the news about the local damage. "It's no one's fault. Sometimes, these things just happen. We're lucky we're okay. It could have been much worse."

"Really? I don't think so," Emma sulked. She knew she sounded like a spoiled brat moaning about the dance being canceled, but it felt like such a letdown. She looked out the window—the sky was perfectly blue and the sun was shining. It was the calm after the storm. But couldn't it have waited to happen over the weekend? Did Mother Nature have to step in and spoil everything the day of the dance?

As disappointed as she was, she knew the rest of her classmates would be just as upset. Harriet called her, moaning: "It's not fair! I slept in rollers all night so my hair would have beachy waves!"

"I wish we could have the dance somewhere else besides the gym," Emma thought out loud. "The storm is over. My dad says it's perfectly safe to go out."

"Go where?" Harriet replied. "Did you read the email from Principal Bates? The gym is underwater. Are we supposed to swim at the dance? And to think of all that cake and ice cream that will go to waste!"

Ice cream! Why hadn't she thought of it before?

"Harriet, I need you to call Izzy and meet me at Freddy's in an hour."

"Emma!" Harriet wailed. "How can you eat at a time like this? The Sadie Hawkins Dance is history."

"No it isn't—not yet," Emma promised her. "I have an idea how to save it."

#

"Freddy," Emma said, barging through the door of the ice cream shop. "We have a terrible predicament." She knew Freddy's had survived five decades of rain, snow, sleet—even a small earthquake—and remained unscathed. The nor'easter had knocked out power in the area, but Freddy had an emergency generator so his ice cream would never melt. The lights were on, and Freddy was polishing the tabletops with a damp rag so they sparkled.

Freddy sat down on a counter stool and stroked his white beard. "Lay it on me," he said. "I've heard it all over the years. What's the problem?"

"Our school gym is flooded," Harriet said.

"Underwater," Izzy added.

"Totaled," Emma continued. "And we were supposed to have our seventh-grade dance last night. That's seventy very disappointed seventh graders."

"Devastated," Izzy piped up.

"Miserable," Harriet sniffled.

"Well, that is a new one," Freddy said. "I've never heard of a sunken gymnasium before. But what can I do to help? You kids need a few pints of Really Rocky Road to cheer you up?"

"Not exactly," Emma said. "We need you to host the dance here."

"Here? Seventy kids dancing here?" Freddy mopped his brow with a dish towel. "That's a tall order, young lady."

Emma walked around the ice cream shop. "If we pushed back all the tables, it would make room for a dance floor." She continued visualizing it. "We could put the chairs stacked up high in the kitchen."

"Don't get me wrong, I'd love to help you and

your friends out, Emma. But I don't think I have the resources for a fancy dance. Who would I get for staff? Or to help me set and clean up?"

"We could ask Jordie and her decorating team to come in and make everything pretty and pink. Luc didn't deliver the supplies, they're all still waiting at Partytopia."

"And I'm sure Ms. Bates, Mr. Goddard, and some of our parents would pitch in," Izzy added.

"A dance needs music, doesn't it?" the owner asked them. "All I got is an old jukebox that barely works in the corner."

"Winston could do the audio and the lighting," Emma volunteered. "He's a whiz at it."

"I dunno," Freddy said. "I've never done anything like this before."

"Pretty please," Emma pleaded. "It's just one night and you could totally save the day. You'd be our hero!"

Freddy leaned back and looked around. "A hero, huh? You really think you could dress this place up and have a dance here?"

"I know we could," Emma said, confidently.

"Then I guess I can't say no," Freddy replied.

Emma threw her arms around him and hugged him. "Freddy, we can't thank you enough. This is going to be the best Sadie Hawkins Dance anyone has ever seen."

#

Emma called Principal Bates to tell her the good news.

"That's wonderful, Emma," Ms. Bates said. "And Austen will pick up the tab for all the ice cream—make sure you tell Freddy to save me one of his root beer floats!"

Harriet and Izzy were in charge of calling in the troops: Jordie and Lyla would bring all the cheerleaders to help decorate Freddy's; Elton, Jax, and the soccer and track teams would help move the tables and chairs and clear the room; and Winston and the school show-choir tech crew would set up speakers and lights. They would all pitch in and help clean up, leaving Freddy's spic-and-span after the dance was over.

That left Emma to fill in the rest of her classmates—with a special *Ask Emma* Urgent News Post. She sat at her laptop and typed:

> Dear Fellow Seventh Graders,
>
> I have some good news—make that some great news. Even though our gym is in bad shape after the storm, we have a place to have an amazing Sadie Hawkins Dance tonight: Freddy's Deep Freeze! Everyone is pitching in to make this dance perfect. So get ready, get your dancing shoes on, and see you there at seven tonight! Please spread the word and make sure everyone knows we're back on!
>
> XO,
>
> Emma

Her dad knocked gently on her door. "So now

you can add party planner to your résumé, eh?" Mr. Woods joked. "I hear you saved the seventh-grade dance by getting Freddy to host it."

"And I hear you asked Mom to marry her over a bowl of Lucky Charms," Emma teased. "We're both very creative."

"That we are," her dad said, smiling. "I also thought you might need a few extra hands tonight at the party, so your mom and I can volunteer."

"Really? You don't mind?" Emma asked.

"Mind? There's a Funky Monkey Banana Split with my name on it waiting at Freddy's. You can pay me back in ice cream—and you know Freddy serves 'twenty tongue-tantalizing flavors every day.'"

"It's a deal," Emma agreed. "Thanks, Dad."

"Oh, and I got your brother to DJ," her father added. "I had to bribe him with a *Star Wars* marathon for the next five family movie nights, but I figure it's worth it."

Emma winced. "Okay. Anything to save the dance."

Now the only detail that was left was Emma herself—in all the commotion over the storm, she hadn't given much thought to how she wanted to wear her hair or what color lipstick and eye shadow would go with her purple dress. She stared at herself in her bathroom mirror: Her nose was sprinkled with freckles and her hair hung in loose blond waves down her back. She remembered what Jax had told her, "Sometimes you think too much, Emma, and you get carried away." Then she thought about what her mom had said about her dad winning her over by being "the realest boy she ever met." She applied just a dot of lip gloss, a hint of mascara, and a touch of powder, letting her natural beauty—and her freckles—shine through. Then she scooped her hair into a low ponytail and tied it with a lavender ribbon to match her dress. It was all simply perfect, and it was all simply *her*.

13

A MAGICAL NIGHT

The doors at Freddy's Deep Freeze were locked until precisely seven o'clock—that's when the long line of Austen seventh graders winding around the block got their first glimpse of the Sadie Hawkins Dance in all its glory.

Emma had decided she would meet Jax there. She'd keep everything cool and casual; the last thing she wanted to do was scare him again. As she walked through the door, what she saw took her breath away. The entire room was draped in pink toile, and pink balloons floated on the ceiling. She couldn't believe this was Freddy's; it looked more like something out of a fairy tale. She had to admit it: Jordie and her cheerleaders had done an amazing job transforming the room into a magical space, and Luc and the Partytopia staff had certainly come through. Winston had strung sparkling lights all along the counter, and music was booming from speakers he had mounted on the walls.

"Isn't it beautiful?" Harriet gushed. She looked like a frosted cupcake in her puffy pink dress with a sheer layer of shimmering sequins sprinkled across the skirt. "I can't believe we pulled this off, Emma. After everything we went through, it's just perfect." Marty was wearing a white suit and pink tie to match.

"Not too shabby, huh?" he asked Emma, tugging on his lapels.

"I kind of expected you two to dress as Superman and Supergirl—but this is much better," Emma joked.

Izzy and Elton also looked perfectly paired: She wore a little black dress with a red sash around her waist, and Elton was in a black shirt and red bow tie.

Everyone looked amazing—so elegant, so put together.

"Make way, make way," Lyla said, parting the sea of students for Jordie's big entrance.

"The queen has arrived," Ty told Emma. "You don't wanna miss this."

Emma stepped aside and watched and waited like the rest of the seventh grade for Jordie's fashionably late arrival.

Finally, she appeared at the door, a vision in bubblegum pink, from her billowing ball gown to her elbow-length gloves to the tiara perched on top of her updo. Winston trailed behind her, proud and perfectly matched in a black tux with a pink bow tie and cummerbund. His hair was slicked back, and his glasses were tucked away in his pocket.

"Winston, you're a vision," Emma told him. "I never would have recognized you."

"I don't recognize me, either," Winston admitted. "But I like it!"

Jordie strolled over to Emma. "I have to hand it to you," she told her. "You saved the dance. I would have been very upset if this custom couture gown didn't have its moment in the spotlight."

"Glad I could help," Emma said.

"Helping is your talent," Jordie told her. "Like mine is singing, dancing, acting—just about everything else."

Emma tried not to laugh; Jordie was a bit full of herself. But telling her she had a talent for helping others made up for it. It's the one thing that truly made her feel fulfilled—just knowing that she had been able to bring so many people together and come up with a way to prevent this magical night from being canceled.

She suddenly spied Jax watching her from the corner by the jukebox. She waved, and he came over, smiling.

"You look amazing," he said. He was wearing a

light-blue, button-down shirt that made his eyes look even bluer, and a purple tie that complemented her dress.

"How did you know what color my dress was?" Emma asked, surprised. "That tie is a perfect match."

"Two little birdies might have told me," Jax said. "You really have some great friends." He handed her a wrist corsage made of delicate purple irises and lilacs.

Emma looked around the room at her matchmaking handiwork: There was Marty and Harriet, arm and arm; Izzy and Elton toasting each other with ice cream sundaes; Lyla and Ty busting some moves on the dance floor; Winston carrying the train on Jordie's gown and grinning from ear to ear; Ms. Bates and Mr. Goddard were standing by the punch bowl chatting; and even her parents looked delighted to be helping, scooping out cups of ice cream with Freddy behind the counter.

"Ya wanna dance?" Jax asked her. She remembered the last time they had danced together, at the Student

Congress after-party, while Maroon 5 performed in the background.

"I loved the iMovie you made," he whispered in her ear as they began to take the floor side by side. Emma looked stunned—how could he have possibly seen it?

Jax read her mind. "I said you had the best friends—they kind of snuck it off your laptop and sent it to me."

Remind me to strangle Izzy and Harriet, Emma thought. *And remind me to change my password!* But she couldn't be angry at them; they had just been trying to get her and Jax back together. Come to think of it, she definitely would have done the same thing herself.

"They figured since you helped them get their dates for the dance, the least they could do was patch things up between us."

"And did it work?" Emma asked, shyly. "Did they patch things up, I mean?" He was holding one of her hands in his and the other was around her waist.

"I never forgot about DC or us, Emma," he admitted.

"Well, you seemed to have a pretty bad case of amnesia."

"I'm sorry I acted weird, but I'm glad you didn't give up on me."

Emma saw her dad dipping her mom on the dance floor. "We Woods are pretty persistent," she said. "I tried everything I could to make you like me again."

"You didn't have to do that," Jax told her. "Because I think you're amazing just the way you are."

Emma noticed the music had suddenly stopped. She heard Luc's voice over the microphone: "And this one goes out to someone you all know: Emma Woods." Bruno Mars's "Just the Way You Are" began playing, and a confetti cannon suddenly went off showering the entire dance floor in pink and silver. Everyone cheered—even Ms. Bates and Mr. Goddard who seemed to be gazing into each other's eyes.

"You set this up, too?" Emma laughed. "How much did it take to bribe Luc?"

"Ten dollars," Jax said, grinning. "And I told Mr. Freddy the soccer and track teams would handle the cleanup. That's a whole lotta confetti."

"Very impressive," Emma said. "You thought of everything—and I had no idea what you were up to."

"I can do sneaky," Jax said. "I learned from the best."

They swayed to the music and Emma rested her cheek against Jax's shoulder. This felt right. *They* felt right together. And Emma couldn't have been happier if she had planned the whole thing herself.

And for once, she was glad she hadn't.

CARRIE'S GUIDE TO THE ULTIMATE SLUMBER PARTY!

Want to throw the most epic party à la the gang at Austen Middle School? Gather your BFFs for a slumber party and prepare to have the night of your life—Ask Emma *style!*

INVITE YOUR GUESTS

Make a potential guest list of five to eight of your closest friends (depending on how much space you have at home) and show your parents before moving forward with invitations. Once they approve, it's time to figure out whether you want to Evite, text, purchase, or make your own invitations. If you want to go the DIY route, an online template with a bright, welcoming border (cute heart or floral patterns are always winners) works perfectly. You can slip the invite into your besties' lockers at school and wait for replies to come rolling in! Always make sure your invitation includes:

WHO: You! The name of the person hosting

WHAT: An awesome slumber party!

WHERE: Your address

WHEN: Date and time, including pickup the next day

WHAT TO BRING: PJs, sleeping bag, pillow, robe, slippers, toothbrush, change of clothes for the next morning. You can also ask guests to bring their fave board games to play, or some homemade snacks to share.

RSVP: A date to let you know if they're in or out for the festivities

CONTACT: An email and/or phone number in case your guests or their parents need to reach you for more details or with questions

Once you finalize your list of attendees, start a group chat and coordinate outfits for the night.

Matching PJs and scrunchies make for the most adorable selfies!

DECK THE HALLS

Or, in this case, your bedroom, basement, living room—whatever locale you're planning on staging your sleepover. Be as creative as you like: Set up mini fabric tents for each guest; string lights, balloons, paper lanterns, butterflies, streamers. Maybe (like Jordie) you want to have a pretty-and-pink theme! You can also set up fun "stations" for girls to do activities, i.e. "The Nail Salon"—a table with assorted polishes for giving one another mani-pedis. (See below for more activity ideas.)

ARRANGE YOUR EATS

Before your friends arrive, prepare an assortment of snacks to nibble on throughout the course of the evening. I recommend placing Cheetos, popcorn, candy, and chips in large bowls to share. Finger foods are also a good choice: mini grilled cheese sandwiches (cut them in quarters); chicken nuggets with assorted dipping sauces; mini pizza bagels; fruit kabobs (chunks of melon, pineapple, and grapes on wooden skewers).

KEEP 'EM BUSY!

You want your partygoers to have lots of things to do over the course of the evening. Here are a few fun ideas:

Blind Makeovers: Set up a station with assorted cosmetics: eye shadows, lipsticks, blushers, etc. One girl is blindfolded and attempts to do makeup on another girl without being able to see how/where she's applying it. After the big reveal (guaranteed to cause giggles), take a selfie!

DIY Pillowcases: For this activity, you'll need a bunch of Sharpie markers, white cotton pillowcases for each guest, and (if you want to get fancy), a computer and printer. You can find some fun images online and print them out on Jet-Pro Heat Transfer Paper. (You iron on the image.) The girls can then color in the images with Sharpies. If you intend to use the cases to sleep on that night, simply toss them in the washer/dryer for a quick spin.

Freddy's Deep Freeze: Inspired by the yummilicious ice cream shoppe in *Ask Emma: Boy Trouble*, set up a station of assorted ice creams and toppings and let your friends make their own sundaes. Or serve up a giant treat for sharing with your entire crew.

JAX AND EMMA'S "KITCHEN SINK SPLIT"

Depending on how many guests are sharing the sundae, you will want to add more ice cream and toppings. This version serves four to six people.

INGREDIENTS

- 2 scoops Cookies and Cream ice cream
- 2 scoops Rocky Road ice cream
- 2 scoops Pistachio ice cream
- 2 scoops Strawberry ice cream
- 2 scoops Banana ice cream

Place all of the above in a large chilled bowl. Top with:

- Hot fudge topping
- Whipped cream
- Chocolate sprinkles
- Rainbow sprinkles

Hand everyone a spoon and dig in!

MAKE YOUR OWN FACE MASKS

Using just a few ingredients you can find in the kitchen, your guests can indulge in some relaxing facials you mix up yourselves. NOTE: Please make sure to ask your friends if they have any allergies before applying masks.

- **THE BYE-BYE-OIL BANANA MASK**: For this soothing mask that minimizes shine, mash up one ripe banana in a small mixing bowl and add in two tablespoons of honey. Add a few drops of lemon juice and stir until all ingredients are combined. Apply on face for ten to fifteen minutes and then rinse with warm water.

- **THE YOGURT-AND-EGG-WHITE MOISTURE MASK:** This one has only two ingredients and makes skin feel oh-so-soft: Combine two egg whites in a small mixing bowl with two tablespoons of plain yogurt. Apply for a few minutes before rinsing off with warm water.
- **A BERRY-FINE MASK FOR CLEAR SKIN:** Lemon juice is a natural astringent—awesome for banishing breakouts! Mash two to three strawberries (stems removed) in a small mixing bowl. Add one teaspoon of lemon juice and apply to face, allowing to sit for ten to fifteen minutes. Rinse off with warm water.

BREAK OUT THE TUNES!

Create a playlist of your fave songs and have a dance party. Like Izzy says, "Wave your hands in the air like you just don't care!" A few of my faves to get you on your feet:

"Girls Just Want to Have Fun" by Cyndi Lauper

"Run the World (Girls)" by Beyoncé

"Happy" by Pharrell Williams

"Firework" by Katy Perry

"I Gotta Feeling" by The Black Eyed Peas

"Party in the USA" by Miley Cyrus

"Dancing Queen" by ABBA

"Can't Stop the Feeling!" by Justin Timberlake

SNUGGLE UP FOR A SCREAM-FEST

Turn out the lights, zip up your sleeping bag, and screen a marathon of scary movies! I'd recommend these PG-13 flicks for a fun freak-out: *The Others, The Ring, The Sixth Sense, Poltergeist.*

PLAY A GAME

"Messy Twister" is a fun "twist" on the popular party game. If you've got the outdoor space, you gotta try it!

YOU'LL NEED:

- 3 cans shaving cream
- Box of assorted food coloring
- 4 large mixing bowls

1. Squirt enough shaving cream into a bowl so it's two-thirds full, then add a couple of drops of food coloring and mix to achieve the colors of the Twister board: red, yellow, green, and blue.

2. Lay out your Twister mat some place you can make a mess: ideally outside on the grass since there will be a lot of slipping and sliding involved and you want a nice, cushy landing. Also, it should be somewhere you can hose or mop down easily afterward (and make sure you have your parents' permission). Ask your girls to bring a T-shirt and shorts or a bathing suit that they won't mind getting "tie-dyed" with colorful stains.
3. Now here comes the messy part: Get your guests in position and begin the game. Everyone will be covered in colorful foam and have the best time ever! Make sure to take pics before you shower off.

AND THE PARTY GOES ON . . .

In the morning, if you have the energy to do so (maybe some shut-eye is a good thing?), gather your buds and make your own pancakes (ask an adult to supervise the stovetop). You could even use some leftover candy/toppings from your Freddie's Freeze Shoppe to dress up your breakfast!

Once your friends leave, be sure to clean up your

home so that no traces of your slumber party remain. That way, your parents see you're responsible enough to host a sleepover and will allow you to do so again in the future. Trust me: After this epic event, you're going to want to plan your next slumber party ASAP.

A *New York Times*–bestselling author several times over, **Sheryl Berk** is most proud of the dozens of books she has cowritten with her daughter, Carrie, including The Cupcake Club and Fashion Academy series. The Ask Emma series is their third collaboration.

A renowned celebrity ghostwriter, Sheryl has worked with Maddie and Mackenzie Ziegler, Jack & Jack, Matthew Espinosa, Zendaya, Britney Spears, and others. Her number-one bestseller, *Soul Surfer* with Bethany Hamilton, was adapted into a major motion picture.

At only sixteen years old, **Carrie Berk** is already a bestselling children's book author, fashion journalist, playwright, influencer, and creator of the style empowerment website, Carrie's Chronicles. She's also proud to serve as a teen ambassador for No Bully.

carrieschronicles.com